LPB
DAWSON, Peter
Run to Goldrock

Run to Goldrock

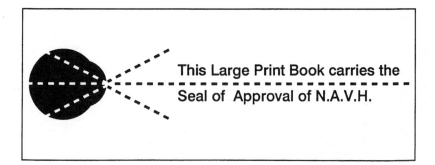

This Large Print Book carries the
Seal of Approval of N.A.V.H.

Run to Goldrock

Peter Dawson

G.K. Hall & Co.
Thorndike, Maine

Published in Large Print by arrangement with
The Golden West Literary Agency.

G.K. Hall Large Print Book Series.

Printed on acid free paper in the United States of America.

Set in 18 pt. Plantin.

Library of Congress Cataloging-in-Publication Data

Dawson, Peter, 1907–
    [Stagline feud]
    Run to Goldrock / Peter Dawson.
        p.   cm. — (G.K. Hall large print book series)
    Previously published with title: The Stagline feud.
    ISBN 0-8161-5733-2 (alk. paper)
    1. Large type books. I. Title.
    [PS3507.A848R8 1993]
    813'.54—dc20   92-44605

I

HE CAME in on the before-dawn train and boarded the stage at Alkali, a tall fine-drawn man carrying a cowhide suitcase and with lean bronzed face, Stetson, waist overalls, and boots definitely marking him as range-bred. Because he took a seat atop the mud wagon rather than one inside with the eight other passengers, Mark Burkitt, the driver, assumed he didn't want conversation. Such was the case. Burkitt mentioned the weather first and got a monosyllabic answer. Then at dawn, with the sun a hot brass ball edging the flat horizon into a cloudless sky, Burkitt made some ripe observations on the discomforts of desert travel; his passenger spoke a sparse-word agreement, nothing else.

So it went, all the way to Dead Horse station, where six fresh relay animals were put in harness, on to Lonesome, where the teams were changed again. The glaring heat and the dust didn't seem to bother

1

the passenger, whose gravity pronounced him too preoccupied with his thoughts to be wholly aware of anything outside them. At Baker's Crossing station, with the northward hills approaching, he remained politely aloof from his fellow passengers during the half-hour stopover in which was eaten a tasteless noonday meal.

Fifteen miles beyond the Crossing, well into the gaunt and barren foothills where the breeze came as a breath from a furnace and whipped the alkali dust in long streams from the wheel rims, the trail's upgrade stiffened and the going slowed. It was while the teams slogged into one of those long climbs that a high-bodied Concord mail coach suddenly appeared around a turning above and came racing down on the mud wagon, its three teams of Morgans at the lope. Burkitt reined his horses quickly aside, booted home the brake, and shook his fist at the Concord's driver as the big coach shot past, smothering its sturdier and less graceful cousin in a fog of dust.

It was then that the passenger was pried from his shell of silence, drawling, "Friend of yours?"

"Him?" Burkitt tongued his tobacco

from one cheek to the other and spat viciously, glaring after the down-going Concord, "Like hell! That was a Mountain coach."

Frank Justice, the passenger, smiled thinly at the venom behind the driver's words. He had seen the legend *Mountain Stages* on the coach's gleaming door panel. The weathered lettering on the mud wagon's side read *Stagline*. Until now he had had every reason to consider the latter name appropriate, for today this stage had traveled the desert and hills with the untiring swiftness of a stag. But that brief glimpse of the coach had made the mud wagon seem ungainly and slow and cumbersome and he felt an unaccountable disappointment, as though his own pride, not the driver's, had been wounded. There was a reason for this. In his pocket was a letter from Paul Le Soeur, owner of Stagline, and much of his daylong preoccupation had concerned that letter. So he was more than mildly curious over what had just happened.

"Acted sort of high and mighty, didn't he?" The question was intentionally prodding, for he wanted more information.

Burkitt put his teams up the trail again

3

before he replied. "They all do, all that Mountain bunch! They're always primed for trouble with us."

"Not enough business for two lines?"

"Hell, yes! But try and tell 'em that."

Frank Justice was for several moments busy taking in the implications of this remark. Finally he asked, "This has happened before, then?"

"Not the same way," Burkitt told him. "But we watch them jaspers. Last week it was a change of schedule. Up till then each outfit had brought up one stage a day. Ours met the mornin' local, theirs the noon express. What did Mountain do but put a stage on each train! So the boss decided to get us up before breakfast to connect with Number Six, the train you come in on, and not fight over the others. Suits me. It gets me in earlier and I don't run the chance of gettin' a cracked skull fightin' over passengers. Damned if I get my teeth jarred loose for the pay I'm drawin'! It ain't no fightin' wages."

"Le Soeur's your boss?"

"Yeah." Burkitt eyed his passenger with a new and somewhat suspicious interest. "Know him?"

"I did a few years back."

4

"Good man to work for," Burkitt said cautiously.

That was the end of their talk. Frank Justice put a couple more questions but got evasive answers. Burkitt evidently thought he'd overstepped in his salty comment on how far his wages went toward buying his loyalty.

However, Frank had heard enough to satisfy him on one point. Paul Le Soeur's letter had offered him a job but omitted any mention of trouble. He wondered idly whether he would have changed his plans if Le Soeur had gone into more detail. In the end he decided he'd have come anyway.

He had been licked, properly cleaned, by a two-year drought. The bank might have extended his note with the right encouragement, loaded as it was with parched grassland and bloated steers. But the weather had been something Frank couldn't fight, something too intangible to gamble against any longer. The gambling instinct was strong in him and he had backed his decision to leave by the knowledge that a loser shouldn't crowd his luck. If the cards went against a man, he should quit the game. That was the way he chose to look on it; he had bought in heavily, had lost, and would get out before he started borrowing.

He saw the aptness of that comparison— as though his ranch had been his take in a no-limit game. Well, it had worked out that way. Probably he should have known it would, for the six thousand dollars he'd put into his brand had come straight from a poker table. He had won that money on a gamble and he now chose to think he'd lost it on another.

He smiled as he looked back across those five years to that night in Trail. He could still feel his eyes smart to the glare of the lamp hanging over the green-felted table and to the fog of tobacco smoke that thickened the stale air of the saloon. Even now he could feel the flow of excitement along his nerves as he saw again the disorderly mound of chips, paper money, and gold that littered the table's center. He had come away from that table a heavy winner, Paul Le Soeur had had a part in that game, had won too. A winning streak couldn't go on forever, Frank decided. Now bad luck had caught up with him, cleaned him, and he was making a new beginning in a new country.

It struck him that Paul Le Soeur might also be having his share of bad luck. Le Soeur, too, might one day be stripped of his easily come-by stake. Then he shrugged the thought away, having nothing more than Burkitt's vague statements to back it. He hoped sincerely that he had the wrong hunch on Le Soeur's luck.

His next hour atop the jolting, swaying stage brought some clear thinking that let him coolly and logically cast aside the remaining shackles of an immediate and disagreeable past, of boredom and futile striving and failure. It put him in a long-forgotten and reckless mood, one that made him ignore the fact that winter was on the way and that the money in his pocket wouldn't even buy him a ticket out. He was young enough to make a new start, barely crowding thirty; he'd always had a liking for new faces, new country, and he'd never regretted the fiddle-footedness that made him even now unsure of what place to call home, whether it would be the Powder River country or that below the Mogollon Rim; lastly, there was always his luck—good or bad, he was still gambling on it. It was due for a change.

The stage's last relays were put in harness at the station below The Narrows a little short of dusk. There the main canyon narrowed and, beyond, the road climbed steeply and deeper into the hills. The last view of the downward desert was shut out. Late fall's early darkness came quickly, totally, for the canyon's high walls left only a thin wedge of the star-brightening sky above. The air grew steadily colder so that a coat was comfortable where it had been unbearable during the day. Burkitt lit his lanterns, but their light was feeble and he drove mostly by feel and his thorough knowledge of the trail.

Tangled as he was with his thoughts, Frank had no way of knowing how much later it was when Burkitt pointed out and downward with the five-foot ash stock of his whip and announced bluntly, "There she is, stranger. Goldrock. The hellhole o' creation!"

Down there, in the bed of a bowl-like valley shut in by tall round-shouldered hills, was a sprinkling of lights, thickest along a single street's stem. The mud wagon was dropping under brake along a winding trail that led down from the high flanking canyon rim. The brake blocks squealed over the jingle of doubletree chains and the creak of harness. Frank, weary from the daylong unfamiliar lurching of the thorough braces, was only faintly interested in the look of the town, for he had seen boom camps before. He most wanted a good meal, a bath and a shave, and some sleep.

They rolled in past a stamp mill and the rosy-glowing high chimney of a smelter, climbing a little, and were on the town's street. Briefly they were flanked by tar paper and board shacks and the white blob of tents graying the darkness. Then, with the suddenness of a blacksmith's hammer striking the anvil, the street became crowded and lighted and noisy, bordered by wide walk awnings abutting false-fronted stores and saloons and cubbyhole offices. The walks were jammed with a restless-moving traffic of people whose talk and laughter and harsh oaths struck up an undertone of sound that even the rumble of passing loaded ore wagons couldn't muffle. Tie rails along the walks were packed with saddle horses and small rigs and a few heavy wagons. The middle of the street was as crowded as the walks, foot traffic mingling with and miraculously coming

unscathed from the jam of teams and saddle animals.

"There's where our trouble comes
from," the driver said presently, nodding
to the right walk.

Frank saw what Burkitt meant. Over a
covered runway backing a long ramp leading from the street arched a sign lettered
brightly *Mountain Stages.* The layout was
impressive, lights shining from the windows of a big waiting room and office
alongside the runway, lanterns beyond
faintly lighting a deep and wide expanse
of open yard backed by sheds and a barn.
Across that space Frank saw a high-bodied
glistening Concord, like the one that had
passed them on the trail, moving into the
runway.

His glimpse of Mountain's yard was
brief. For, a moment after he spoke,
Burkitt lunged suddenly to his feet, snarled
an oath, and flicked the eleven-foot lash
of his whip so that it exploded over the
rump of his off-leader. Frank instantly saw
the urgency of the move. A buckboard had
swung out into the stage's path from immediately beyond the slanting ramp. The
mud wagon was too heavy to be turned
quickly. The whip was intended to swing

the leaders out, along with weight on the reins.

Burkitt was a trifle late. The leaders collided with the nearest of the buckboard's team of bays. The off-lead animal reared, forefeet tangling with the buckboard's harness. Then came a rumble of iron tires rolling across planking. Burkitt shot a glance back over his shoulder to the yard runway and yelled, "Jump!"

Back there the big mail coach Frank had briefly glimpsed was now rolling fast down the ramp into the street. Instead of turning his teams to avoid collision, the Concord's driver came straight on. His teams trotted smartly past the mud wagon's rear; his front wheel cleared nicely. Then, in a jarring slam, the hub of his rear axle locked with the mud wagon's wheel rim.

Lazily almost, the mud wagon tilted up and over. Frank jumped clear. Burkitt, thrown off balance, fell astraddle the tongue as the near wheel animal went down. The mud wagon landed on its side with a heavy grating thud. Inside, a woman passenger screamed shrilly time and again.

Ignoring his horses, Burkitt leaped the tongue and wheeled on the stalled Concord. His arm cocked back, snaking out the long lash of his whip. He made his throw expertly, upward. Two feet of the whip's thong curled about the upraised arm of the mail coach's driver. Burkitt's weight leaned against the whip. The Concord's driver left his high perch in an ungainly dive, arms out-thrust to break his fall. Frank saw Burkitt lunge in at the man; then the mud wagon's sky-aimed side hid the drivers from view.

Shouts along the walk swung Frank's glance over there. He was in time to see half a dozen men coming down Mountain's ramp. Three of them carried short heavy clubs. By the time he called a warning to Burkitt, the first of them had rounded the mud wagon's rear.

He had a choice to make. A man passenger was having difficulty swinging open the overturned stage's heavy door. The woman screamed again. Yet Burkitt's sharp cry from behind the stage decided him. He wheeled around there, shouldering aside one man and throwing himself on the back of another in the act of swinging a club down on Burkitt, who was on his knees. He collided with Burkitt's assailant, pushed him sprawling, and wheeled in time to duck the vicious stroke

12

of a club in the hands of a man behind. Standing spraddle-legged over Burkitt, he swung hard at this one, catching him full on the point of the jaw and dropping him with the looseness of a half-empty sack of grain. Then the others were on him and Burkitt was standing unsteadily alongside, trying to protect himself.

Frank reached down for the club of the man he had dropped. While he stooped, a powerful blow struck him deep along the back. Coming erect, he used the upsurge of his body to put drive behind his club. He caught the man who had hit him full in the chest, slamming him back hard against an axle brace of the mud wagon. The rest of Mountain's crew, seeing two of their number down, hesitated.

It was the exact moment to force home this small advantage. Frank threw his club hard at the nearest man. The club's heavy handle arched in under the man's hastily upraised arms, catching him in the mouth. He cried out in pain and staggered back, spitting blood, as Frank lunged in at him.

"Hold it, you highbinders!" came a strident voice from out on the street.

That shout took Frank's glance briefly out there. Pushing through the gathering jam of spectators came a solid high-built man with a rugged handsome face and dark eyes aglint with visible anger. A low-slung holster along his right thigh shouldn't have marked him particularly in this crowd where many men wore weapons openly, but the thonged-down slant of the weapon was what immediately took Frank's eye.

"Hold it!" the man shouted again, and then was clear of the onlookers and within two strides of Frank.

Mountain's crew retreated several steps, surprisingly, before the man's approach. The one Frank had last struck down crawled out of the reach of Burkitt's boot as it swung at him.

Burkitt, hatless, his forehead bleeding from a long gash, breathed, "Brice, I'm through! Right now, by God! I want my pay!"

"You'll get it!" the newcomer, Brice, drawled dryly. He was about to add something, still eying Mountain's crew, when suddenly his right hand streaked up along his thigh. That hand was a blur for a split second, settling finally at his hip in an exploding stab of powder flame.

The shot beat heavily back from a false-fronted building across the street. One of Mountain's crew cried out sharply and staggered out from behind one of his companions, a half-drawn gun falling from his hand as he reached over to clench a bleeding forearm.

Brice held his gun loosely, muzzle down, and drawled, "Any other takers?" His question brought no reply. He motioned meagerly with his gun to the overturned mud wagon. "Help those passengers out."

The Mountain men moved sullenly in toward the stage, one of them reaching up to help the badly frightened woman passenger climb aground. Brice, meantime, came closer to Frank. He holstered his gun with the same swift ease he had drawn it.

"Thanks for the help, friend," he said. Then, louder, "All right. Turn it back on its wheels."

The stage, empty now, shortly lurched upright under the heaving of Mountain's sullenly submissive yardmen.

When the luggage and express spilled from the back boot was loaded once more, Brice went over to the woman passenger and Frank heard him say, "Sorry this happened, ma'am. If you'll get in again, we'll take you to your hotel."

The woman made some objection Frank didn't hear and indignantly turned and walked away through the crowd. After that, Brice's attention went up to the driver of the mail coach, once more on his seat and tightly clenching his shoulder, which had evidently been sprained in his fall.

"You, Hoff! One more break like this and I'll personally see to it you get the beating of your life." Brice spoke mildly, but he was big enough to back his word to almost any man. "This was rigged, wasn't it?"

The driver up there said sourly, "Hell, no! Your man blocked my way. It was his fault."

Brice, turning to speak to Burkitt, found that his driver had gone. He shrugged, called "Clear the street, Hoff!" as the driver of an ore wagon, helplessly blocked by the tangle of traffic, bawled oaths over the heads of the dense crowd.

Presently the street's jam thinned and Brice climbed up to the seat on the mud wagon's roof. Frank joined him.

As the teams got under way, Brice

16

looked across at him and smiled broadly. "I shouldn't have stopped your fun. You were goin' great."

"Good thing you did," Frank said.

He noticed Brice's expert handling of the reins and was once again impressed with the cool efficiency of this man. Brice was taking the fight casually, almost as a matter of course. From Burkitt's talk he decided that Brice was Stagline's manager. If so, Paul Le Soeur had picked a good man. Brice's manner back there had lacked any touch of arrogance, yet he had nicely driven home the quick turn of affairs Frank had started. He could have killed the Mountain crewman trying to draw on him; instead, he'd wounded him with a shot Frank knew hadn't been a lucky one, and thus completed his thorough cowing of the rival crew. Frank had the feeling that he was going to like Brice. He also had the hunch that his work with Stagline, if Le Soeur still had that job open, was going to be more interesting than it had looked in the beginning.

Stagline's yard was fronted by a long slab fence with a wide gate at the far end. Beyond the gate stood a plain frame shack flanked by a platform. The light of the one lantern on the platform didn't cut the shadowed rear of the yard, so that Frank could make out nothing of what lay back there. When Brice braked the stage, the platform was within an easy step of the door. Two passengers who had come on to the yard got out and a crewman came out of the door of the shack to climb onto the back boot and unload it.

Frank was about to ask for Le Soeur when Brice called to his crewman, "Boss in?"

"Gone home to supper," was the answer. "Said he'd be back later."

So Frank waited until his suitcase was handed down and decided to go back downstreet to the hotel. He was leaving the platform when Brice came over and said, "Much obliged for the help, stranger. They'd have pulled this rig apart if it hadn't been for you."

Frank said, "See you again," and went out the gate.

A cot, one of four in a small back room at the Palace Hotel, cost him five dollars for the night. A shave at a barbershop and a bath out in the yard behind it came to a dollar and a quarter. The bath consisted of his standing in a tarp enclosure while water dripped down onto him from holes punched in the bottom of a five-gallon syrup can; he enjoyed it as much as any he could remember, for the air had a bite to it and the brisk toweling that rubbed the chill from his long frame seemed to sweep clean his mind of its last lingering doubt over his having come here. He felt good. By the time he handed over another two dollars for a plain but filling meal, he felt even better. He knew these boom camps and how much it cost a man to keep clean and fill his belly. Trail had been a boom camp and he'd had some fun there. Goldrock was bigger, lustier, tougher maybe. But he liked it and his hunch was that it was going to treat him well.

He supposed he should wait until morning to see Le Soeur. But he was impatient to find out how things stood. So, finished with his meal, he went back up the street, feeling the abrupt change that was so in contrast to his life of the past five years. Those years had been solitary ones, little to his liking. This was better, having to shove your way along a crowded walk, smelling the whisky-laden air before the mouth of a saloon, pushing harder than the next man when he tried to shoulder you off the walk. The din from the saloons was inviting, but he didn't stop. That could come later. Maybe Le Soeur would break out a bottle to welcome him. He hoped so, for he felt the need of a drink—only one.

He wished he knew Le Soeur better. Their acquaintance back in Trail had been too brief, too suddenly ended, to suit Frank. Le Soeur was older, but Frank had seen in him that same strain of fatality and the disregard of what tomorrow might bring that was such a strong part of his own make-up. Le Soeur had had a good laugh, a quick smile, honest eyes. He hadn't been much of a talker. Neither was Frank. They'd get on.

Stagline's yard was dark, the platform in shadow except for a faint wedge of lamplight that shone out through the half glass of the shanty door. Frank supposed that the door led into the office.

He had to grope around in the darkness to find the platform step. His knock on the door went unanswered. He was about to turn away, deciding Le Soeur had already gone, when he became faintly curious over the light inside. So he opened the door.

Light from a bracket lamp disclosed a small office. Across the room was a plain pine filing cabinet and shelves crowded with ledgers. There was a deep leather chair set obliquely to the far corner. Immediately to this side of the door stood a red-painted roll-top desk with a swivel chair behind it.

All this Frank saw in a brief sweeping glance that settled finally on a leg and a boot showing from behind the big leather chair in the corner. A needlelike prickling of excitement traveled his spine as he crossed to the chair. He pulled it aside. He was staring down into the half-smiling face of a gray-haired man. But the glistening dark stain that marred the dull surface of the boards under the man's grizzled head betrayed the look of peaceful repose on his face.

This man was Paul Le Soeur. He was dead.

II

SAM OSGOOD was more reluctant to face this day than any within his memory. He'd been up most of last night, seeing to arrangements for the funeral and going over Paul Le Soeur's legal affairs. His friend's death had hit him hard; so hard, in fact, that he hadn't the nerve to face Belle last night.

The tragedy that had struck so suddenly to wipe out the hard-bought happiness of the two people nearest and dearest to him was hard to realize. Paul Le Soeur had brought him here following the death of his wife a little over a year ago and it was due to Paul and his daughter, Belle, that he hadn't gone to pieces. Now, the sense of his own loss having become bearable, he was feeling the weight of a second. It didn't matter now that the past year had brought him a small lifetime of success in the law business; all that did matter was that Paul was dead and that he was taking on a solemn trust. That trust was his duty to Belle Le Soeur.

He stood at the window of his second-floor office, staring sightlessly down onto the street, sober under the prospect of having to become a foster father to a girl he loved as much as he would have his own daughter. He and his wife had been childless, making the tie with Belle all the stronger. He wondered what he would say to Belle and decided that whatever he said wouldn't matter; Belle couldn't help but know his feelings.

He glanced at his watch. Nine-forty. Belle was coming at ten. His eyes went back down to the street, not seeing it, and in this moment he was a frail stooped man looking older than his years, which were fifty-four. His hawkish face was kindly even under its grave and flinty expression. He had had a hard life and now he wondered if he was to find peace in this world. It was something he'd never thought about before. He almost envied Paul Le Soeur.

He willfully stopped the bleak run of his thoughts and really saw the street for the first time in the long minutes he'd been standing here. His window looked out on an ever-changing scene, yet one that was basically the same. Slater, across the street, had just added a new front to his saddle-shop. The Mercantile was a clash of color now that George Selden had loosened up enough to afford a coat of bright red paint. The walks were crowded, as usual, and the saloons were doing a full-out business that was the same now as at midnight or three in the morning. Up-canyon he could see the slopes dotted with the shaft houses of the mines, their pyr-amided muck dumps, and the tracery of the winding roads that led to them. Down those trails rolled the many ore wagons, converging into the common line of the street and finally to the stamp mill and the smelter below town. The placers far-ther up the canyon were out of sight.

His glance took in the broad rectangle of Stagline's station-yard farther up the street and opposite, and he immediately thought of Frank Justice and last night. Jim Faunce, the town marshal, had sent a man after him to bring him to the yard. He hadn't believed what the man told him until he pulled the tarp aside and looked down at Paul's body where it lay in the far corner of the stage office.

There had been a few bad minutes when he was filled with a killing lust directed at the stranger sitting handcuffed in the chair behind the roll-top desk, for Faunce had calmly informed him that this stranger was Paul's murderer. Luckily he'd kept his head and asked a few questions.

The stranger himself had reported the shooting, so Faunce said; some poppycock about having discovered the body when he called to see Le Soeur, as Faunce put it.

No, there had been no one in the yard to verify his claim. Then Osgood had caught the stranger's name, Frank Justice. It had meant something to him and he had silenced Faunce curtly and talked to Justice himself. Then Ed Brice had arrived to settle matters conclusively. He had told them about the stage accident on the street two hours before, had told them how Justice had pitched in and fought the Mountain crew almost single-handed. Justice had claimed that his gun was in his suitcase at the hotel. Faunce had sent a man down there and found the gun, its barrel dusty, the cylinder loaded but for an empty chamber under the hammer. Faunce insisted that Justice could have used another gun. But when his prisoner produced a letter from Le Soeur, a letter offering a job, Faunce had reluctantly taken off the handcuffs and grumbled a sullen apology.

Later Osgood, Brice, and Justice had taken the body down to the undertaker's. Justice had stayed on with Osgood while Brice had returned to the yard to meet Belle. During the next hour the lawyer had had the chance to size up Paul Le Soeur's friend. He was satisfied with what he saw, a tall quiet man who held no resentment

25

toward Faunce or anyone else over the night's misunderstanding.

Osgood had asked Justice to come to the office this morning. He had been too worried and busy to explain his summons. That explanation would come in a few minutes now, after Belle and Justice arrived.

A step on the outside stairway turned him from the window. He answered the knock on the door and it opened on the man he had been thinking about, Frank Justice.

Frank said, "Too early?" and Osgood told him, "Not at all. Come in."

When Osgood had indicated a chair that faced his desk and had taken the one behind it, he offered a box of cigars. Frank took one and his match lit both their smokes. Osgood searched a drawer and took out a folded paper, Paul Le Soeur's last will and testament.

He said, "You know about Paul's will, of course."

Frank shook his head. "Should I?"

"Didn't he mention it?" Not until he'd spoken did Osgood remember having read Paul's letter to Justice last night, so he added, "Of course not. But hadn't he written you before?"

"Only this once. I came right on, since a bank had just sold five years' work out from under me."

"You're broke?"

Frank smiled thinly. "Dead broke."

Osgood's faint smile had nothing to do with Frank's. He said, "Get ready for a jolt, Justice. You know, don't you, that Paul has been looking for you since you gave him that money?"

"He didn't say so."

"Whether he said it or not, he's combed the country for you. He always considered that six thousand you gave him a rightful debt."

"It wasn't a debt."

"Paul chose to think so."

Osgood leaned back in his chair, pulling at his cigar. He was curious about this man, having expected to meet a gambler. But Justice didn't have the look of a man of the profession; he seemed more like a typical 'puncher whose experience with the cards totaled no more than the ordinary run of cut-throat bunkhouse gambling, red dog and stud and draw. He wondered how he could lead up to the subject of that game in Trail, one Paul Le Soeur had never tired of telling.

27

He asked, "Have you known Paul long?"

"No. I saw him that once, in Trail."

"Never before that?"

Frank shook his head. "Never before or since."

Osgood was obviously surprised. "I thought you knew him well. I also thought you'd be a gambler. You don't look like one."

"Never made a business of cards," Frank said. "All I know is the tank towns."

"Trail wasn't a tank town. And that game wasn't penny ante." Osgood waited a moment, hoping his visitor would go on. Then he understood that this man Justice wasn't in the habit of talking much and saw that he'd have to force the conversation. "According to Le Soeur's story, you drove a herd to Trail and sold to the mines. How did you happen to tangle with Matt Phenego?"

"He ran a saloon. I had money and a powerful thirst. When I drink I usually wind up in a game."

"Paul said you lost the first night and went back the second and cleaned house. What put you onto the marked cards?"

"My luck was good, but still I lost. The cards were the only answer."

"So you got a deck and learned the markings." Osgood was still having to keep the talk rolling. "How did you manage that?"

"One of the aprons was a trustful soul and thought I was taking the deck back into the game."

"So you won twelve thousand that second night because you knew the cards. Where did Paul come in?"

"On the last hand. I had Phenego beat and bet all my winnings. Phenego thought he'd steal the hand by raisin' so I couldn't touch him. I was shy five hundred on the call. Le Soeur tossed in the money for me."

"And Paul was a total stranger to you?"

Frank nodded. "He knew it was a crooked game and saw his chance to make Phenego eat crow. He wasn't doin' it for me. I didn't count."

"And Phenego let you take the money? Wasn't there something about you using a gun?"

"It didn't get down to cases. I'd had it in my lap for the last hour and showed it when Phenego wanted to toss Le Soeur out for hornin' in."

"That was a lot of money to win at one sitting."

"It wasn't so much the money as the fun we had robbin' Phenego."

Osgood said evenly, "Paul was that way too. He never attached the proper importance to any large sum. He had his fun spending it, though."

"He seemed like that kind," Frank drawled.

Osgood drew gently on his cigar, squinting into the smoke and studying Frank covertly. His visitor spoke casually of a thing that had taken on great importance to Paul Le Soeur, and in turn to Osgood himself. Le Soeur had never tired of telling about the game in Trail and of Frank, who had, with his help, exposed Phenego's crooked game. Le Soeur's share in Justice's winnings had set him up in business and it was logical that he had always spoken highly of Frank. Osgood was pleased to see that his friend hadn't made a wrong judgment.

"Paul tried to return that money," he said. "He's tried for five years."

"It wasn't intended to be returned. It was his, for keeps."

"How did you get him to take it in the first place?"

"Wrapped it in a cigar box and paid

30

a kid a quarter to take it to him. By the time he got around to lookin' for me, I was on the way out."

Osgood said, "It was like Paul never to forget that debt, careless as he might have been with his own money. And he hasn't forgotten it, Justice."

Frank shrugged and settled farther down in his chair.

Abruptly Osgood asked, "Justice, do you know that Matt Phenego is here in Gold-rock?"

"No!" softly.

Osgood noticed that Frank's gray-blue eyes were no longer pleasant-looking. A surface glint had come to them, giving them the smoky quality of a thunderhead-clouded sky. "More than that," Osgood stated, "Phenego owns the other stage line, Mountain."

Frank gave a barely audible whistle and his face went sober, "So it's me that brought all this trouble on Le Soeur."

"Don't look at it that way," Osgood said. "It was Paul's own affair. But he couldn't fight Phenego. He wouldn't use the same tactics. Three weeks ago one of his stages was held up and lost its Wells-Fargo chest and a sack of mail. There was three thou-

31

sand in the chest. Paul paid the loss back out of his own pocket. Since then he's had a battle to keep Wells-Fargo and other gold shippers from transferring their contracts to Phenego's line, and a postal inspector came in to look things over."

"Why didn't he hire guards?"

"He did. Phenego bought them off. We can't prove it, but we think that's what's happened."

Frank smiled, and his expression lacked all amusement. "This is beginnin' to sound like fun! I'll take a job, any one you've got. With just pay enough to buy me grub."

Osgood's grizzled head moved in a slow negative. "You'll never get the chance, Justice, much as I'd like to see it. It's poor business to continue the line in the face of things as they stand. Phenego has money. Stagline hasn't. About every cent to Paul's name is invested in the line. We're selling out."

"Maybe that's sense," Frank agreed.

"You won't think so when you hear the name of the buyer."

"Phenego?" Frank asked quietly.

Osgood nodded. "Phenego. He's been after the business for months now. We think he's given us all this trouble to crowd us out, to pay Le Soeur back for his share in helping you win that game in Trail. Each month he's tried to buy. At each of Paul's refusals his price has come down a thousand dollars. Now he gets Stagline for a song."

"I'm sure sorry," Frank drawled. "Le Soeur shouldn't have had to buck my troubles along with his own."

"He didn't mind. In fact, at times I think Paul enjoyed this kind of a fight. What hurts me more than anything else is that he swore he'd never sell to Phenego. Now we're forced to, much as we hate going against his wishes. His daughter needs the money. So do you, I take it."

"Me? What's this got to do with me?" Frank queried.

Osgood smiled thinly. "I told you to get ready for a jolt, Justice. Here it is. Paul Le Soeur finally found a way of paying back his debt to you. His will leaves you a half interest in Stagline. You and Belle Le Soeur are partners."

III

FRANK'S LONG frame stiffened in the chair under the impact of the lawyer's words. He drawled, "Something's wrong here, Osgood. You can't have it straight."

"It is." Osgood couldn't help but smile. "You may have been broke a minute ago, but you're far from it now. Today, at the latest tomorrow, you'll have five thousand dollars."

Frank appeared not to have heard him, frowning at a thought he didn't word for a long moment. When he did speak, it was in a soft drawl, "Then it's a safe bet Phenego killed Le Soeur."

Osgood's hands lifted from the desk in an outspread gesture of helplessness. "He's the logical one to suspect. But we don't have proof."

"We don't need it."

As those flat-toned words struck across to him, Osgood noticed the instinctive brief lift of Frank's hand along his thigh. Frank was wearing no weapon, but Osgood needed nothing so tangible to seal his understanding of the move.

It made the lawyer shake his head. "No, Justice. It would never do. There's a law here. Jim Faunce. You met him last night. He was put in office by votes Matt Phenego bought. There's not a shred of proof as to who killed Paul. If Phenego's responsible, one of his men did it. Go after him and you put a noose around your neck. He'll have an alibi, never doubt that. And he's got influence here. You wouldn't live long enough to get out of the country."

"But neither would he," Frank reminded him.

Again the lawyer's head moved in a brief negative. "Let it rest, Justice. Take your money and get out and . . ."

The sound of a solid boot tread blended with a lighter step came in off the stairway outside. Osgood stood up, suddenly remembering Belle Le Soeur's coming. In these last few minutes with Justice he had forgotten what he was going to say to her. A knock had sounded on the door and he had answered it before he could think back. Then the door was opening on Ed Brice's tall solid shape and Belle's slender one.

As the girl came into the room, saying, "Hello, Sam," her rich low voice steadied

35

the lawyer. He came solemnly across the room, looked at her a moment, then gathered her into his arms in an impulsive unashamed way. Words would have been meaningless, even wrong, at that moment. In the strong pressure her arms gave in answering his embrace, he knew that Belle understood his feelings. When he stepped away and told her, "Belle, this is Frank Justice," he was himself once more.

As Frank nodded to the introduction, Osgood having stepped aside so that he could get a clear look at the girl, a heretofore unknown chord of interest was struck deep within him. He was momentarily too confused to say the things he knew he should be saying, for something in this girl's looks attracted him so strongly he was unsure of himself. Her hair was ash-blond in striking contrast to deep brown eyes that strongly reminded him of her father's. But there ended any likeness between father and daughter. Le Soeur had been a short heavy man with rugged, almost homely features. This girl was tall and willowy; broader of shoulder than most women. Her finely molded face had more of character than beauty in it—the mouth was generously wide, the nose uptilted a trifle—yet Belle Le Soeur was as beautiful a woman as he could remember. And he found it odd in thinking of her as a woman, for she appeared to be a girl in her early twenties; he decided finally that it was something about her eyes, what seemed a deep underlying understanding, that gave that impression of maturity.

He found himself saying, "I'm sorry for what happened last night."

She gave him a long open look before she murmured, "Dad wanted so badly to see you again."

Then Ed Brice was helping her off with her coat and the strained moment had passed. Her words had definitely made Frank welcome.

He was awed by her serenity. Her fresh loveliness gave no hint of inward grief; there had been no sign of tears or hysterics in her meeting with Osgood. Frank soberly told himself that Belle Le Soeur was something out of the ordinary.

Presently Osgood had pulled a chair in for her to the desk corner opposite Frank's, and Ed Brice was sitting on the window ledge and the lawyer was saying, "I've just finished telling Justice about the partnership, Belle. About the sale, too. He—"

"I'll sign the whole thing over to you," Frank interrupted, speaking to the girl. "Your father—"

"Dad wanted it this way," Belle Le Soeur insisted. "It's as it should be, your sharing. If it hadn't been for your money, he could never have gone into the business he always loved. And don't feel sorry for him, any of you." Her head tilted up and there was a glow of pride in her dark eyes. "His life was the way I hope mine will be, full, rich, meaning something to those who knew him. It ended as he'd have wanted it, quickly, before old age crippled him. Don't let's pity him."

For a long moment following her words, an acute stillness filled the room, crowding out the street sounds. Then Sam Osgood was pushing his chair back noisily across the bare board floor, leaning over to pull open the bottom drawer of his desk, saying, "I have the payroll ledger here. If you all agree, we'll give the men a week's notice."

At the window Ed Brice nodded his agreement and said, "The change-over won't lose anyone his job. Phenego's keepin' 'em all on."

38

Now that Frank could think clearly back upon the things he and Osgood had been talking of before this interruption, he was bothered by something he found hard to define. Then he was wording that thought without being quite aware of what it was. "Aren't we goin' at this thing a little hasty?"

"What thing?" There was a faint yet striking edge of belligerence in Brice's tone.

It was commanding; for what Frank remembered of last night's meeting had given him a deep respect for this man even without his gun, which Brice wasn't wearing now.

"Sellin' to Phenego," Frank told him. "First off, Le Soeur wouldn't want it. He—"

"Dad had one fault," the girl put in. "He had few enemies. But he never forgot his reasons for hating those few. This isn't the time for us to keep alive an old grudge."

"Ma'am, this Matt Phenego may be the one who shot your father," Frank bluntly reminded her. His face darkened in embarrassment as he saw her wince at the words. But now, he felt, was the time for pressing home his point. "Maybe we could hold out against him; hit back."

39

"You saw what happened yesterday, Justice," Brice said sharply. "That accident cost me a driver, the best one I had."

"No man who won't fight for his outfit is worth his salt, Brice. Burkitt was licked before he tangled with Phenego's bunch. He was soft. Hire a few gents with chips on their shoulders, ones who'll look for trouble instead of dodgin' it!" Having started this, Frank was unwilling to give in before he'd made his point.

"Then we *would* be licked." Brice smiled wryly and shook his head. "Phenego's spoilin' for an out-and-out fight. No, you'd better take the offer I got you."

Seeing Frank frown his puzzlement, Osgood put in, "Phenego has been after Brice to work for him for months now, Justice. We owe it to Ed that Phenego agreed to buy the line at all. Remember, he doesn't have to. He could stand by and watch us waste away what little is left."

There was something here Frank didn't understand. It was that intangible something that robbed these three of a strength of will he knew they all possessed. Because Brice seemed so cocksure, because Frank disliked the inference that Brice had been dealing with Phenego, however honorable his intentions, a strong stubbornness was mounting up in him that now dwarfed Brice's former stature in his regard. He had never been a man to give in easily, as Osgood and this girl and Brice seemed to be doing.

But, instead of too hastily speaking his thoughts, he began warily, "I can see both sides, Le Soeur's and yours. But who is Phenego? A man, isn't he? A man like the rest of us. If he can fight, why can't we? In a camp like this men come cheap. Why not go out after Phenego the same way he's after us? Hire enough men to guarantee your gold shipments. Go out after more business. Put a stage on every train. Back your play with guns if necessary. But don't give up like chickens runnin' at the sight of a cowbird's shadow!"

It wasn't often that Frank broke from the habit of being sparse with words. Finished now, he sensed he had said too much. The girl was staring at him with wide-open eyes, as though he were slightly mad. Brice's blunt handsome face had darkened. Osgood sucked at his dead cigar, unaware that it wasn't lighted.

It was Brice who answered. His words

were accompanied by a low derisive laugh. "What do you know about stagin', Justice? You act like we hadn't been tryin'! You say to hire men. What with? We're nearly broke. You say to use guns. If we do, what chance have we got against Phenego's bought law? As for goin' out after new business, we're losin' more today than we can hold. I tell you, Stagline's finished!"

"And where'll you be if we sell out?" Frank drawled. He was definitely over his awe of this man. Brice wasn't reacting to his expectation.

Brice seemed surprised at the question. "Where would I be? Runnin' the line, of course."

"Then you don't lose a thing, do you? Phenego keeps you on. Miss Le Soeur loses practically everything. She gets maybe enough to keep her for four or five years, nothing else."

Brice smiled and looked down at the girl sitting close to him. "Belle needn't worry," he drawled, reaching out to lay a hand on the girl's arm in a gesture that was full of meaning and held its own answer.

Sam Osgood sensed the antagonism building between these two men. "I can see both sides, too, Justice. But, believe me, there's been nothing to make me think we shouldn't take Phenego's offer."

Frank looked at Belle Le Soeur, "What do you really think?"

His question startled her. "You must know what I think. But . . ."

"But what?"

"I'm sorry we're having to go against Dad's wishes."

"Then why do you?"

"We haven't a chance otherwise."

Rebellious before the combined wills of these three, Frank was groping for a way to force his own decision. Finally he thought he had it. "If you're anxious to get out, why not sell to me?" he asked. Osgood gave him a quick look that made him add, "I don't have the price of a week's board right now. But there are men back where I came from who know a good thing when they see it. Give me four or five days to go back after money. I'll buy Stagline."

Brice stiffened. "You're loco, Justice."

This man was used to giving orders and being obeyed, Frank recognized that, yet drawled, "I'll forget you said that!"

His tone, the sudden glint of anger in

his eyes, made Osgood put in, "Ed, lay off! You have nothing to do with these decisions." He took a handkerchief from his pocket and blotted his forehead. The room wasn't warm, but he was perspiring. He saw the flare of antagonism on Brice's face and added, more mildly, "We have a lot of respect for your word, Ed. But let's cool off. If Justice can get the money to buy the outfit, I'd a damn' sight rather sell to him than to Paul Le Soeur's enemy."

"What does Justice know about staging?" It was obvious that Brice would stubbornly hold to his honest convictions.

"I know horses," Frank stated. "And I know a little about men."

"You're a gambler!" Brice said coldly. "I've nothing against the breed, only that now's no time to take risks. You'll be bankrupt inside a month. I won't have anything to do with it."

"No one said you had to."

Stagline's manager stood suddenly erect as those words struck him visibly, almost like a hard blow. His big fists knotted and he glared across at Frank in open hostility. "So you're firin' me!"

"You just said you wouldn't go in on

anything as harebrained as this." Frank shrugged. "I don't see as I've had anything to say about your stayin'. You quit, Brice."

A slow twisted smile came to bring back the ruddy good looks of Ed Brice's face. "You've called the turn, Justice," he drawled. "Now I'll call one." He looked down at the girl. "Belle, I start working for Mountain, beginning now. Phenego's held the job open for me. And I'm against Stagline, meaning Justice. I'll make a personal guarantee that there won't be a Stagline wheel rollin' the trails inside a month!"

"Any money to lay on that?" Frank asked. He couldn't let that flat challenge go unanswered although he realized he should be trying to reason with Brice.

"None. I'm a poor man. But I've got my brains and a pretty strong back to lay on it." Abruptly Brice seemed to sense the futility of further argument. He said quietly, "So long, Belle," and stepped around her and went to the door, not hesitating there but going straight out, closing it softly after him.

Frank grudgingly admitted that that final show of well-curbed emotion had almost made him like Brice again. Strongly he felt that he had met a man he would rather have had with than against him.

IV

THEY LISTENED to the receding pound of Brice's boots going down the outside stairway. Finally it faded altogether. Now in this following silence they could hear, almost feel, the heavy rhythmic pound of the ore crushers below town at the stamp mill. The stillness grew so tense that it seemed a tangible thing pressing in on them. Belle Le Soeur sat staring fascinated at Frank, as though seeing him for the first time. Sam Osgood deliberately inspected the cold ash of his cigar and said quietly, "He meant that, Justice."

"So I take it." Frank's look went to the girl. "Will you give me an option?" He caught her so preoccupied that he had to repeat himself, adding, "Or would you rather think it over?"

This time she found a firm grip on her emotions. Her face took on color, but she spoke low-voiced, intently, "Can't you see what you've done? Ed was trying to be fair, to help me! Now you've . . ."

"You're not losing by it," Frank reminded her. "Either you'll have ten thousand of my money a week from now or you can take Phenego's."

"Five thousand," she corrected.

Frank moved his head in a negative. "Ten. Your share's worth that. And it's a good buy for me at that price."

His insistence seemed to rob her of her anger. She gave Osgood a helpless look and the lawyer said, "We're all het up now. Let's wait till we cool off. I'd think the whole thing over, Belle." He came around the desk and took her coat from the rack by the door. Still looking a trifle bewildered, she let him help her on with it. Then he was saying quietly, "I'll stop around for you at two. Don't worry about this."

She lingered a moment in the doorway, looking back at Frank as though there was something she wanted to say. But in the end she turned without a word and went down the stairs.

The click of the door latch was a signal for Sam Osgood to say sharply, "How serious are you about this, Justice?"

"Plenty. I hate a bad loser."

"It's a big risk to take to get even with a man."

47

"Who said anything about gettin' even? I'm going into business."

Frank's caustic tone reminded Osgood of several things, chief of which was that this man, a comparative stranger, had reacted with typical indignation to the death of Paul Le Soeur; it was the way he, Osgood, might have reacted had he been younger and hardier. Yet his admiration for this Frank Justice was tempered by all he knew about Matt Phenego, his power, his devious ways and the heartless quality in him that made him crush and push aside all opposition regardless of the methods used. He admitted that he liked Frank; also, that he feared the consequences of Frank's rashness.

Thinking this, he took the most direct way that occurred to him of discouraging the decision. "You may be willing enough but I'm here to protect my client's interests. What guarantees have I that you can buy Stagline?"

"None." Frank shrugged. "Like I said, there are some men who might go in with me. I wouldn't know for sure until I talk with 'em."

"They'd be quick enough to see that you were working off a grudge."

"That don't count," Frank drawled. "What does is that Phenego's price on the outfit makes it a good proposition, a sound investment. Providin' it's run right, it ought to pay well."

"And you think you can run it?"

"I can try."

Blocked along this line of reasoning, Osgood turned to another. "You've just lost us the best staging man in this country, Justice." His look was angry and his tones crisp and indignant. "You've thrown a scare into a girl who's had all the tough breaks one person should be asked to take. You're asking me to sanction a scheme that's harebrained, that's bound to fail if you go ahead with it. My duty to Belle means I can't let it happen."

"Can you sell to Phenego without my go-ahead?"

"No."

"Then you might as well forget it."

Osgood tried to stare his man down for a moment, then turned to reach for his hat. The faint hint of a smile touched his face while his back was turned, for he had to admit that Frank had nerve. Facing Frank once more, his expression was flinty, severe. He took out his watch and looked

49

at it. "In that case, I have no choice. I can spare you an hour. We'd better get down to the yard and start picking up the pieces."

"What pieces?"

"The ones Brice left. It's a cinch he took some of your men across to Mountain with him. The down-stage is due to leave in thirty minutes. You'll be lucky if you have a man to drive it."

If he expected this threat of difficulties to come to influence Frank, he was wrong. Frank merely nodded, put on his Stetson, and came to the door.

They had nothing to say to each other in the brief walk that took them to Stagline's yard. Sam Osgood was feeling a little ashamed of himself. Regardless of the need for caution where Belle's affairs were concerned, he felt envious of Frank, recognizing in him the purposefulness, the will to act, that he himself lacked. So accustomed was he to weigh carefully his every action and word that he found it refreshing to meet a man so direct who seemed to have the ability to back even so rash a decision as this. Last night he had heard of Frank's part in the stage collision; he didn't doubt that more violence lay in the near future. And, strangely

50

enough, he had decided that Frank Justice was capable of meeting it. That decision irritated him. He felt that he was somehow betraying Belle Le Soeur in even mildly tolerating this sudden turn of affairs.

Frank's first glimpse of Stagline's yard showed him things he hadn't been able to see in the darkness last night. His range-bred eye approved the orderly arrangement of the compound. Fronted by the long slab fence on the street side to the east, the lot was better than a hundred feet deep. Two long steep-roofed sheds opened inward on its south side, one sheltering a mud wagon like the one he had ridden in yesterday. Behind those sheds ran a line of tightly built stables with ample loft space for the storage of hay. A big corral and a blacksmith shop took up the yard's back boundary, while to the north, behind the office shack, was a bunkhouse. This shelter, better than most of the town's makeshift buildings, he later learned was one reason for Paul Le Soeur's having had his pick of men. A crewman living there could save a sizable chunk of his pay that would otherwise have gone toward renting proper quarters somewhere else in town.

All this Frank took in briefly before his glance settled on the group of four men gathered before the bunkhouse door. Instinctively he knew the reason for this gathering that had taken Stagline's crew from its work; Ed Brice had been here.

"Only four," Osgood said. "There ought to be seven." He led the way across there.

He was direct, first informing the men that Frank was the new owner. He saved them the awkwardness of singly introducing them, merely mentioning their names: "Harmon," the brawny squat-framed man in the leather blacksmith's apron; "Bob Aspen," a lanky youth, the yard hostler; "Yates," a wrangler whose duty it was to keep the sixty-odd animals comprising Stagline's remuda in condition; and "Fred Cash."

The last-mentioned, an oldster with a tobacco-yellowed beard, was the only one who made any response beyond a nod. He announced tersely, in a croaking voice, "We're shorthanded as hell, mister! But we're with you. Brice was gettin' too big for his pants."

"Who went with him, Cash?" Osgood asked.

"Dennis and Closson and Billings."

"Then we're shy a driver."

Old Cash nodded and an eager light came to his eyes. He shifted from one foot to the other in such a way that Frank noticed he was a cripple. "I could wheel 'er down, Osgood."

The lawyer shook his head, smiling briefly as he glanced up at Frank and told him, "Cash used to drive for Butterfield."

"Damn' right I did!" the oldster flared. He slapped his crooked right leg. "Just because I got a bum pin, Brice claims I'm finished." A pleading look came to his eyes. "Osgood, all I need is a chance to prove I ain't!"

Sam Osgood was again moving his head in a negative when Frank drawled, "Why not? Have we got anyone else to take the stage down?"

"No," Osgood said. "Walters is the only driver left and he's bringing in the upbound from Alkali."

"Then give Cash a try," Frank put in as the lawyer hesitated.

When Osgood saw the amazed, almost worshipful expression that crossed Fred Cash's face, he decided to keep his opinion to himself. He saw at once that Frank was making a good beginning toward winning the loyalty of the crew and he was sportsmanlike enough not to argue against it. Cash had long been crowing of his years with Butterfield; Ed Brice and the others had taken him as a joke, keeping him on for odd jobs only because of Paul Le Soeur's insistence. After all, Osgood reasoned, it was up to Frank to make the decisions from now on.

Harmon, the blacksmith, said, "There's some more bad news. Night before last Hank Williams was seen comin' out of Phenego's office at the saloon." He added, for Frank's benefit, "Hank owns the station down at The Narrows. If he's so minded, and if Phenego lays enough on the line, he can refuse us our relays."

"He'd sell us out?" Frank queried.

"Williams'd sell his birth certificate if it was worth anything . . . and if he had one," Fred Cash drawled.

Frank was trying to remember the look of the country below The Narrows as he had seen it yesterday. Shortly he said, "Then we'd better get ready for him. Can we spare a man to go down there in a light rig and throw up a rope corral? Seems

I remember a small meadow a mile or so below the station."

Young Bob Aspen offered eagerly, "I could do it. There's an old tent up in the loft. Yates, you could bring horses down."

Yates, the wrangler, tilted his wide-brimmed hat farther back on his head. "Sure," he agreed. "It could be done. We'd have to haul feed, though." He eyed Frank levelly to ask, "What about this deal Brice has been talkin'? Sellin' out to Mountain?"

"It's not going through," Frank stated, including them all with his glance. "Be on the lookout for new men, good ones. Another driver to spell Cash here wouldn't hurt. Two more should be at The Narrows. And you're short a man here, aren't you?"

Harmon said, "We'll double up on the work till things get rollin'." His broad face took on a smile, revealing white strong teeth. "This's more than we expected, boss. I reckon we'd all have quit rather than work for Phenego."

Several minutes later, in the office, Sam Osgood let out his breath in a long relieved sigh. "You've made a good start," he said. "Wonder how long it'll last?"

55

"We'll make it last."

The lawyer's open regard held for another moment. Then, on sudden impulse, he was saying, "Justice, I've made up my mind."

"On what?"

"On what I'm to advise Belle. Ten minutes ago I was ready to take your offer on buying her out. Now I'm not so sure." A shrewd light tempered by a smile was in his eyes. "I'm just selfish enough for her to want to see her make the best deal possible. Maybe you're the man to pull this outfit up by its bootstraps. I'm going to wait a little longer before I commit her to anything."

"That's not good enough," Frank drawled. "If we wait, we're licked. We ought to begin today, now, on this thing."

Osgood was puzzled. "You've already made a pretty fair start."

"Let's say I have. But there are some other things that need doing. For one, I ought to see Matt Phenego."

"You ought to what!" Osgood said explosively.

Their talk drifted on. They argued, Osgood heatedly, Frank with patience. Instead of the hour he had promised, Sam Osgood remained at Stagline's office until ten minutes before the time set for Paul Le Soeur's funeral. He would have forgotten even then if Frank hadn't reminded him of it.

Shortly after noon a misty rain settled like a filmy shroud down along the canyon. Belle, alone in the house that sat far back and above the street, watched it come. Her eyes were moist as she thought of her father's body being lowered into the ground on such a dismal day, and now she could no longer hold back the grief she had stubbornly kept from showing last night and this morning.

By two, when Osgood knocked gently on the front door, she gave no sign of the bad hour just past. She welcomed him wordlessly, with a thankfulness that came of not wanting to be alone. She let him wrap a light blanket snugly about her legs after she'd stepped from under his umbrella into the buggy he'd hired for the occasion. They had gone a good way along the faintly marked lane that led on up the slope toward the cemetery before either of them spoke.

Then she said quietly, "I'm not afraid any longer, Sam."

He reached over and put a hand on hers and once again she found comfort in his nearness. When she thought of the old times, those far-gone days before tragedy had struck so deeply, it nearly made her cry again. She could remember her father and Sam in those days as two carefree young men in a less forbidding country; she could even remember her mother, the faint perfume of heliotrope she always wore, and a ride much like this out into the country from town . . . only that day there'd been snow and the sun was bright and in the buckboard bed behind the seat was a Christmas tree they were taking to a homesteader family.

"Sam, I'm going to cry," she said.

"You've been needing that, Belle," he told her, and the touch of his hand tightened.

But now it seemed the tears wouldn't come. They climbed on up the lane and rounded a shoulder of the hill and she saw the rigs and saddle horses tethered to the picket fence that ran around the small graveyard.

She saw Frank Justice as she was stepping down out of the buggy. He stood beyond the group of people by the newly turned earth of the grave, tall, straight, bareheaded, and evidently hoping he wouldn't be noticed. Sight of him quickened the slow beat of her pulse and she was suddenly glad that he was there.

A few bouquets lay against the bank of earth beyond the plain board coffin. Sam Osgood, standing beside her, quietly mentioned the names of the people who had sent them, stripped the plants in their homes to bring them. Then Parson Rutledge's gaunt shape moved to the head of the grave and his gray head bowed over his clasped hands that held the Bible. As he began speaking, simply, gravely, she caught only the tone of his words. The picture of Paul Le Soeur was before her, not the father she'd known these last toiling years but the younger man whose kindness and gentleness was blended with a strain of recklessness and a joy of life. Then, strangely, she was thinking of that tall man standing beyond the mourners, Frank Justice. And in that moment she knew why she had liked him even against her will; she had read into his make-up that same restless urging that had driven her father on into new country, the same strong loyalties, and the will to fight for a principle. She knew that it would be easy for her to give in to this Frank Justice, to agree with what he said and did. And she definitely drew up a barrier against that, reminding herself that his wishes ran counter to hers and Osgood's and Brice's.

She didn't know the exact moment Ed Brice stepped soundlessly in alongside her and put a hand through her arm. She only knew that he belonged there; but too, she knew that she hadn't missed him until his late arrival. Even so, she was thankful for the firm support of his arm when Rutledge had finished his brief words and the men, her father's friends, stepped forward to lower the coffin into the ground by its ropes.

As it sank out of sight beneath the lip of the grave, she turned away. And, turning, she saw Frank Justice again. His eyes were on her, gravely, and he didn't look away. His glance somehow helped her through the next few moments when she heard the first shovelful of earth fall hollowly onto the coffin. She had been dreading that, knowing it might wring a cry from her; but because this tall silent man's eyes were on her she didn't flinch.

At the buggy Brice asked, "Would you like me to ride down with you, Belle?"

"Sam will take me," she said.

Afterward she didn't know what impulse had prompted that answer. Ed Brice had the right to be with her, even before Sam Osgood, for Ed was the man she was to marry. But in this moment she wanted to be alone, as alone as she could be with Sam Osgood and his knowing silence. Ed would have wanted to talk, to comfort her. She didn't need that.

They were nearly home when Osgood said, "I almost forgot, Belle. Justice wanted to know where he could get some flowers to send. He didn't like it when I told him a man couldn't buy any in town."

She gave him a direct look, asking, "You like him, don't you, Sam?"

"He's got a way with him. You should have seen him bring that crew around. They're for him."

"So are you."

The lawyer tilted his head in a sober nod. "I might as well admit it."

"You want me to sell out to him then?"

61

"No. I want you to stick with it, Belle. That man will see this thing through."

She murmured, "I thought you'd decide that."

"I'll need your consent, Belle."

An almost inaudible sigh escaped her. "You have it."

V

MATT PHENEGO'S Paradise invariably reminded Ed Brice of a different and a softer life, one he had briefly glimpsed in the days he was beginning his staging experience on the coast. The saloon's main room was big and barnlike, but there ended any similarity between it and Goldrock's other entertainment establishments.

Somewhere in Phenego's nature lay a flair for showmanship. It was evidenced in the lavish use of red and gold gilt paint, in the upholstered chairs at the poker layouts, in the curtained booths and the ornate twelve-lamp crystal chandelier that centered the room. The Paradise was a promise of what was to come if Goldrock ever became the town the promoters now claimed it to be. A bar manned by five aprons ran the entire length of the left wall. Facing it from across the room at the front were gambling layouts—faro, dice, blackjack, and poker. Beyond ran heavily curtained booths, small rooms where exclusive patrons could gamble freely, drink unmolested as much as they wanted, or eat passable meals that were the best the town offered.

Phenego's master touch was a life-size oil painting of a reclining Venus that hung high over the center of the long bar's mirror. Paradise housemen had been known to accept tips from new arrivals who wanted to meet, during her off hours, the percentage girl posing behind the glass. And many a man a little the worse for drink had bought glass after glass of the raw liquor Phenego's aprons served while staring upward at the picture in hopes of seeing evidence of life in it. Phenego freely admitted that his Venus had paid for herself many times over.

Tonight, at this after-supper hour, the Paradise was noisy and smoke-fogged, tainted with the smell of stale beer, tobacco, and whisky. Brice somehow relished the lusty, near-bawdy scene as he sauntered back through the crowd jamming the space between bar and gambling layouts. His big heavy frame nicely topped those of most of the men in the room. He was handsome enough in a rough way to attract the glances of the percentage girls. One even approached him and thrust her arm through his with the invitation, "Have a drink?" But he politely disengaged his arm, said, "Later maybe"; and continued on toward the crowded dance floor at the rear, where couples shuffled awkwardly to the thrumming beat of a three-piece orchestra.

Brice was a man to take the eye, in the same way Frank Justice could never pass unnoticed in any crowd. He gave the impression of being a strong man, physically bigger than most, and with an habitually impassive set of countenance that was painstakingly schooled. It was to Brice's credit that most men thought him a sound thinker; only on rare occasions, as in Osgood's office this morning, did he ever talk too much or give way to his unruly temper to destroy that impression. This was a weakness and he guarded against it with all his stubborn will.

Recollection of that brief session of the

morning laid a sterner than usual look across his face tonight. It was that look that made the houseman stationed at the entrance to the roped-off dance floor step respectfully aside without waiting to find out the nature of his business. The man even nodded to a door at the back of the floor and said, "He's alone."

Approaching that door, Brice's face underwent a change. Its stern cast faded and was replaced by a look faintly uneasy. His knock was firm but not loud, and he gave a slight start at the sound of the deep booming voice inside that answered it.

Matt Phenego was seated in the chair behind his polished mahogany desk. His glance briefly took in Brice's entry, then dropped to some papers on the desk before him as Brice quietly closed the door. He seemed oblivious to Brice's presence for several moments, during which he made a notation on one of the papers and put it in a drawer of the desk.

When he looked up finally, dark eyes scowling from under heavy grizzled brows, he snapped, "You're late," definitely in the way of a man addressing an underling.

"There was lots to do at the yard." Brice's tone was respectful.

"How many men did you bring with you?"

"Three. A driver and two helpers."

"What was the matter with the rest?"

Brice gave a small shrug. He was uncomfortable under this caustic questioning, also a little irritated. "Call it loyalty to Le Soeur."

"Le Soeur's dead!"

Phenego's glance sharpened, as though the thing he was most interested in was catching Brice's reaction to his clipped statement. In this moment he was every inch the domineering brutal man who had fought his way to the top rung of a crooked ladder by means of treachery and greed and heartlessness. A compact big-boned man with heavy shoulders and a barrel chest, he had not been dragged down by advancing age. His hair was graying. Aside from that he was as physically able as he had been at thirty, in his prime. The most outstanding thing about him at this moment was the way his dark eyes seemed to stare deep into Brice.

Feeling the impact of that stare, Brice drawled, "I reckon they're thinking of the girl too."

"What about Justice? How did they take the changeover?"

"Haven't heard yet."

Phenego examined Brice speculatively over a brief interval of silence. Abruptly he stated, "You're soft on that girl."

Brice's solidly handsome face colored. "I'm goin' to marry her."

"Then how can you work for me?"

"I've told her how things stand. Now that Justice has horned in . . ." He was lost for an explanation, uncomfortable before the saloonman's scrutiny; and now a certain stubbornness and pride in him surged visibly to the surface and he added, bridling, "Leave her out of this."

"We can't." Phenego's voice was positive. "I want a man who'll work his guts out for me all the way, who'll fight."

Brice smiled meagerly and drawled, "You can't complain yet. We're agreed on one thing. We both hate Justice's guts. I'll go all the way with you in beating him to contracts, in cutting rates from under him, in beating his schedules. I'll fight him if he asks for a fight. But"—he paused on that word, giving it emphasis—"I won't go in for bushwhack or robbery! That's your line. It's been your line ever since you stopped Le Soeur's stage three weeks ago and took that Wells-Fargo money."

Phenego seemed about to explode. But abruptly a change came over him and he said intently, almost patiently, "Brice, would you believe it if I told you my men didn't hold up that stage, that I don't know who did?"

"Better check up on your crew," Brice drawled.

"I mean it." Phenego's glance didn't waver. "I didn't hold up that stage."

"Then it's because you didn't think of it," Brice said. "As for Justice, I'll knock his pins out from under him without bushwhack or robbin' his stages. I'd prefer to do it that way."

"Now would you?" Phenego drawled, and he seemed to have forgotten the other as his voice took on an edge of scorn. "Supposin' that isn't good enough for me?"

Brice shrugged. "Then I'm not your man."

The saloonman's glance fell to Brice's thigh, to the horn handle of the gun that rode low there. "You wear that thing for looks?" he scoffed.

"No," Brice breathed softly. "To use . . . when it's needed."

Phenego's face colored. "I want to break

that Justice, to see him get down and crawl!"

"So do I. But not your way, Phenego, nor for your reasons."

The saloonman's look was stony and his eyes clouded over with anger running high in him. Then gradually came a change, the breaking of some inner resolve through the surface of his emotion. It softened his face, made it almost pleasant. He said, "All right. You call the deal on your end of things. Go after his business, undercut him on rates, anything. When you're through with him, toss him to me."

Brice seemed relieved. "Suits me. Anything else?"

When Phenego shook his head, he turned and started to the door.

But Phenego did have something else on his mind. It showed in the immediate worried expression that crossed his face the instant Brice's back was turned. He hadn't wanted to mention it, but as Brice reached for the doorknob he did. "Anything new on last night?"

Brice looked over his shoulder quizzically. He didn't reply for a long and, to Phenego, strained moment. Then, "Not a thing, boss, not a thing. I put you to bed. Should there be anything else?"

There was faint irony in Brice's tone. Phenego ignored it. "Keep me posted," he said. "And on your way out tell one of the boys to get hold of Jim Faunce and send him in."

When Brice had gone, Phenego's worry was more apparent. He lit a cigar, but the next five minutes saw him too preoccupied to keep it alight. Instead, he chewed it nervously. By the time Jim Faunce appeared, the thing that was on his mind had robbed him of even his look of sureness.

Facing the town marshal, he made a futile effort to regain a measure of his hard and domineering manner. Sight of Faunce invariably irritated him. He was inclined to be abrupt with the men who worked for him, as he'd been with Brice. But whereas he thought Brice thoroughly capable, he knew Jim Faunce to be a weakling; and he had no tolerance for that breed of man, regardless of the fact that he often found them useful. What he had on his mind tonight made his irritation stronger than ever. Yet, for the first time in his year-long dealings with the marshal, he attempted now to conceal that feeling.

"Have a cigar, Jim," was the way he greeted his man.

Faunce took a cigar from the proffered box. His long thin face showed no expression beyond momentary surprise over this unlooked-for gesture. Always a dour and silent man who seemed to perpetually nurse some deep grievance, he showed Phenego nothing of his inward run of thoughts.

Phenego rarely used patience; he came directly to the point, "Any ideas on who shot Le Soeur, Jim?"

The marshal's pale blue eyes swung sharply up, then away; his match, held before the cigar, burned down almost to his fingers before he drew on it and flicked it out. "Not a glimmer, Matt," he drawled. His glance abruptly strayed back to Phenego and this time didn't waver. "You kiddin'?"

"No, damn it!"

An expression of wonderment came to Faunce's bony face. "You must've been crocked!" he breathed, putting clear emphasis on the second word.

"How come?" Phenego's tone was sharp now.

"I came straight down here as soon as

71

I could get away. You weren't around. They said Brice had taken you across to your room earlier. So I went over there and found you. Cleaned your gun and got your coat off." At the gathering fury on the saloonman's face, he hastily added, "Hell, you needn't worry about me, Matt!"

All the dislike Phenego felt toward the man crowded to the surface. "Get out!" he muttered. And, as Faunce hesitated, he repeated explosively, "Beat it!"

The closing of the door behind Faunce sealed a feeling of acute dread within Phenego. Yesterday had been one of those rare days when he broke a long-established rule, that of never touching whisky. It had happened before and it was always the same. After going months without tasting a drop, the urge in him became too strong to be denied. Yesterday, shortly past noon, he'd broken open a bottle. He'd finished that one and another before his memory failed him. What had happened after that he had no way of knowing; it was always that way the day after—his memory a blank beyond a certain point. This morning he'd wakened in his hotel room, his clothes on, lying on top of the blankets.

His daylong worry over who took him there and put him to bed made him nervous and irritable.

Now he knew the answers, or some of them. Brice had put him to bed. Faunce had later found him lying there, dressed, his gun needing cleaning. Slowly, having tried to sidestep the obvious answer, Matt Phenego was faced with but one conclusion.

He had killed Paul Le Soeur last night.

He swore soundly and wheeled around in his chair to open the small black safe along the wall. He took out a bottle of rye whisky. In the act of tilting it to his mouth, the motion of his hand abruptly froze. Then, cold fury strong on his face, he brought the bottle down in a solid swing against the safe's sharp corner. It broke, spraying the carpet with splintered glass and liquid. He stared down at the stain on the carpet with unseeing eyes, his breathing labored.

In that moment he was as sick of his own company as he'd ever been. He stood up and lit his dead cigar with a match that wavered. Then he went out into the saloon's main room.

VI

ONE EYE squinted to the upcurl of the cigar's smoke, Phenego paused at the dance-floor entrance to glance lazily over the crowd that jammed his saloon. He listened to the slurring rhythm of Slim Sullivan's piano and could tell by the beat of it that Slim was hitting the bottle again. This did nothing to improve the sharp edge of his temper. Because of his own battle against the whisky habit, he insisted on sobriety in an employee.

He said to the houseman standing at his elbow, "Tell Sullivan to see me in the morning," and sauntered over toward the nearest dice table.

For several minutes he stood watching the play, noting with satisfaction the dexterity with which his houseman made four consecutive throws to his point. At each win the house took in a five-dollar gold piece. The customer finally turned away without a word and headed for the bar, and the houseman said idly, "Dull evenin'."

Near by, Jim Faunce sat in the lookout

74

chair of a faro layout. Phenego caught the marshal's glance once and was uncomfortable under it. But he didn't immediately move away, his pride too stubborn to show Faunce his nervousness. When he did turn and start across the room a touch on his arm stopped him. He swung around to face a man whose freckled sun-reddened face, wide hat, boots, and waist overalls proclaimed him to be one of the rarities of this boom camp, a 'puncher.

"You again!" Phenego said, looking down at the man.

"Yeah, me again." The 'puncher looked beyond Phenego to the faro layout and called derisively, "Doin' your work for you, Faunce!" There was open scorn on his face as he stared Faunce down. Then he drawled to Phenego, "If we had a decent law around here instead of that cheap tinhorn sport, you'd put up the ante damn' sudden! Where's my money?"

Phenego was more amused than irritated. He was reminded of a banty rooster he'd once seen tackle a big Leghorn. This Ned Stiles was a small bowlegged man with red hair and the temper to go with it, cocky in the way of most small men.

"See me when I've got more time," Phenego said evasively.

"How about my time?" Stiles bridled.

He went on to say something else. What it was Phenego never learned. For at that moment his attention had strayed to the swing doors up front. And through those doors came a man's high shape; he recognized it over the span of five years and at once the room's sounds dropped away. It was as though he and Frank Justice were alone in the room.

He told the houseman at the dice table, "Get rid of him," nodding to Stiles. "Get Cliff Havens and Roerick. Tell 'em to stick close to me." He started out through the crowd toward the front of the room. Behind him he was aware of his houseman saying, "On your way, bum!" to Stiles.

He was within two strides of Frank before Frank's even gray-eyed glance picked him out from the crowd. If he had expected his approach to bring any surprise, he was disappointed. Frank's slim smile was enigmatic, faintly arrogant, as Phenego came up to him and said, "Long time no see, Justice."

They stepped over to the bar, Phenego

shoving a man aside to make room. "Buy you a drink?" he asked.

Frank shook his head and Phenego was uncomfortable under his glance. Frank's smile still held as he drawled, "You look older, softer, Phenego."

Matt Phenego was remembering that other time when this man's smooth half-insolent drawl had goaded him into a show of temper. He wasn't going to be caught that way again. He matched Frank's smile with a guileless one of his own. "And still the same sucker I always was. What's on your mind?"

"Does there have to be anything?"

There was a strong but hidden under-current of hostility between these two, casual as their words were on the surface. It was as Frank had expected it might be. He had given his visit to the saloon some deliberate thought and left his gun in the office at the yard, purposely, not wanting to give Phenego the chance of crowding him into using it. He was wary now of the things he wanted to say. He understood presently that Phenego had spotted him before approaching, for two men, housemen by their looks, pushed in to the bar close beside Phenego.

The saloonman said, "I understand you're settlin' down here."

"Thinkin' of it," Frank admitted, "on certain conditions."

"Such as?"

"How the business goes. Maybe you heard I've gone into business."

"So they tell me."

"Any objections?"

Phenego's answer was a brief shrug.

"So we aren't going to get along," Frank said, smiling thinly as he drew a silver dollar from his pocket. He spun it into the air, catching it dexterously. "Phenego, I own a half interest in Stagline. At your price it's worth five thousand. Get yourself five thousand and I'll match mine against yours."

Phenego frowned, trying to see what lay in back of this sudden dare. He was irritated as Frank again lazily spun the coin. "Why should I?" he asked finally.

"You wanted the outfit. Here's your chance to get my half. Then you can buy out the girl."

"If I lose?"

"They say you're a gambler."

Phenego's glance narrowed. "What are you gettin' at, Justice?"

78

"The price to buy you out."

"Buy my stage outfit?"

Frank nodded.

Phenego gave a tight-drawn smile. "No you don't."

"All right, you won't gamble. How about a thirty-day option on Mountain? Name your price."

"Nor that either," Phenego drawled.

Frank frowned, giving the saloonman a direct stare. "Why not?"

"You aren't sellin'. Why should I?"

"I'll sell if your ante's right. Ten thousand is about half what our outfit's worth."

"Le Soeur was offered more to start with. I aimed to be fair."

Frank detected a faint irony in the man's voice but let it go. "Twenty thousand will buy us out. Or you can take my offer of thirty for your outfit."

Phenego whistled softly. "That's temptin'! But don't you reckon there's enough business for us both?" He looked over his shoulder and saw Cliff Havens and Ben Roerick, his housemen, bellying up to the bar close by. Beyond them Ned Stiles was approaching. Sight of the redhead put an edge to his voice as he added, "Or do you want to hog it all?"

79

Frank stood looking down at him, pressing home the difference in their stature. "Come down to cases, Phenego. You aim to push me out if you can. I don't push easy. One of us is goin' to get hurt. To save a few broken skulls, I'm makin' you a fair offer. Take it or leave it."

Ned Stiles, alongside Phenego now, said querulously, "Phenego, quit the stall. I want that dough. Forget the extra change and call it two hundred even."

Frank's first look at Ned Stiles showed him an angry and harassed man, a man in a tight spot. He didn't know what the redhead was letting himself in for by this interruption; yet he could guess, and at once liked Stiles for standing up to it. He turned his glance to Phenego in time to see the saloon-owner push out farther from the bar.

Phenego gave Frank a long smug look, finally asking, "So I'm to take it or leave it, Justice?" Without waiting for an answer, his glance went to Stiles. "And you want me to quit the stall, eh?" Amusement touched his eyes but not his impassively set face. He lifted heavy shoulders in a shrug. "Anything to accommodate, gents." He jerked his head to his housemen at the bar, stepped quickly backward, and said, "Toss 'em out, Cliff!"

His order was intended to gain his men the advantage of surprise. As far as Frank was concerned, it did, drawing each move of the succeeding few seconds to a detailed slowness.

Stiles had obviously been expecting trouble. Hard on the heel of Phenego's words, the 'puncher reached to the bar and picked up a near-empty quart whisky bottle that stood there. Holding it by the neck, he wheeled in alongside Frank, a rash grin streaking his face, drawling, "Let's make it tough for 'em, friend!"

Havens and Roerick moved over toward them instantly. Havens, almost as tall as Frank, reached to a hip pocket and his hand came out fisting a leather blackjack. Phenego's move of backing quickly out of Frank's reach had telegraphed a warning through the crowd that brought a quick hush all the way to the room's margins.

Then Ned Stiles threw the bottle. It sailed squarely at Cliff Havens' head, making the man dodge sideward and off balance against the bar to avoid it. As he dodged, his boot caught on a support of the polished brass bar rail.

Frank instantly took advantage of the man's break in stride. He feinted with his left and threw a hard right that Havens ducked and took on the shoulder. Suddenly Havens pressed in, balanced on his toes in the way of a knowing fighter. His head was hunched down between powerful shoulders. He swung on Frank viciously, and his blackjack caught Frank low at the base of his neck on the left side as he was dropping his shoulder. The blow hurt deep down in Frank's thick shoulder muscle and quickened the upward striking of his right fist as he took a step back from the houseman.

Havens had counted on his blow to end things. When it didn't, he brought his guard up and tried to lunge back out of Frank's reach. He was an instant too late. Frank's left struck deep into the pit of his stomach, doubling him over. Then a stiff looping right straightened Havens out rigid, on toes. Frank hit him twice more as he stood that way, both times on the jaw. Havens' head rocked him side to side. Then, seeing Ned Stiles stumble close by and go to his knees before the rush of the other houseman, Frank snatched the blackjack from Havens' loose grip, wheeled, and threw it hard.

The shot-filled leather struck Roerick on the cheek. He gave an involuntary grunt of pain and lurched sideways. Stiles, on the floor, thrust out a boot that tripped him and sent him falling hard backward into the fringes of the crowd.

Frank helped Stiles to his feet and they turned doorward. The crowd, making a game of this, closed in on Roerick and blocked his way so that he couldn't follow. Matt Phenego, standing down the line of the bar, showed his disgust at the unexpected outcome of the fight. Then he saw another houseman emerge from the doorward fringe of the crowd and unexpectedly confront Frank.

A heavy gold ring on the middle finger of the houseman's swinging fist reflected bright light to give Frank a split-second warning of the coming blow. He rolled with the punch as it slammed hard in at the base of his jaw. He brought his knee up in a hard drive as the man closed in on him. He heard the breath sough out of the man's lungs in a hoarse groan and then he swung hard for the face. His

83

fist connected in a knuckle-aching blow. He had a quick glimpse of a contorted bleeding mouth as his assailant went down. Then he and Ned Stiles were pushing along the narrow lane that opened through to the doors. One backward look showed Frank the crowd closing in behind them.

They shouldered quick out of the doors and onto the walk and Stiles said urgently, "This way!"—heading up the walk past the barker's stand and into the jam of people off there. Ten paces farther on, the crowd had swallowed them. At the sound of shouts behind, Stiles grinned up at Frank, rubbed his skinned knuckles, and drawled, "We make a pretty fair team."

They both laughed. Presently, when they were sure they weren't being followed, they slowed their walk, breathing hard. Stiles said, "Goin' anywhere in particular?" When Frank shook his head, the puncher added, "I know where we can get some java that don't eat the bottom out of the cup. A girl I know makes it."

"Sounds good. Lead me to it."

They left the upstreet limit of the walk and soon were passing Stagline's darkened yard. Abreast the gate Stiles said, "He called you Justice. You wouldn't be the gent that took over this outfit today?"

"The same," Frank said.

Stiles' face was pleasant even for its sober set. "The word about Brice quittin' got around pretty fast. He ain't no kid in knee pants. Neither's Phenego. Look out for 'em." There was a return of his smile. "That scrap did me more good than the dinero I was there tryin' to collect."

"Phenego owes you money?"

Stiles nodded. "He shortchanged me on some cayuses I sold him. Now there ain't time for me to drive in more and get set for the winter."

Frank deliberated this bit of information along with his impulse to like this man, knowing little as he did about him. It prompted him to say, "We've got some spare bunks at the yard. Want to use one?"

"A job? Brother, I'd crawl from here to Alkali for the right kind of work!"

"Then be at the yard in the mornin' at five."

"I'll be there at four, just in—"

Stiles' sudden handhold on his arm pulled Frank to a halt. He looked down to see the redhead's face set bleakly, his stare directed ahead along the street.

Looking up there, Frank saw a tall wide-shaped figure turning off the walk onto the porch steps of a small frame house.

That man's shape was vaguely familiar, but he wasn't sure until Stiles breathed, "Brice! That lets us out."

The man's lifeless bitter tones made Frank ask, "He's callin' on this girl you mentioned?"

"Yeah. One day last week he beat hell out of a drunk that pushed Helen off the walk downtown. Took her home afterward. Don't mean nothin', I reckon." He tried to speak lightheartedly, but his casual tone lacked conviction. "Well, there goes our coffee."

The door to the house opened to outline momentarily a girl's slender shape before Brice went in through it. Then it closed and Stiles turned slowly and they started back down the walk.

They didn't speak for several moments. Frank sensed that Ned Stiles was more than mildly interested in the girl back there in the neat white-painted cottage. Remembering the way Brice had stood beside Belle at the cemetery this afternoon, his arm in hers, struck up a slow burning fire of irritation in him. Brice's visit to the house back there gave him a new insight of the man's character, for until now he had respected Stagline's ex-manager for his loyalties and the stubborn will that hadn't broken from principles he thought sound. This was different, this betrayal of Belle Le Soeur, unless there was some other explanation than that Brice was paying this other girl his attentions. Frank sincerely hoped there was for Belle's sake.

He drawled, "We men sure do suffer, Stiles."

The earlier smile broke through the grave set of the 'puncher's face. "Don't we! But I can't get it straight in my mind. She seems to like the guy, talks about him a lot. You'd think he'd be satisfied with the way things are lined up for him. They claim he's all set to marry the Le Soeur girl."

"It'll blow over, Stiles."

The 'puncher shook his head. "I ain't so sure. Helen's young, too young to know her own mind. She's got a brother that ought to be lookin' out after her. But he's watchman on a closed-down mine up in Jimtown and don't get down here often." He paused a moment, his ruddy face breaking into a smile. "Brice better go

87

easy. Roy Moreford's about the size of an ore wagon. A big jasper with more fun and less brains in him than a sheep dog. But he's strong on Helen. I had a sweet time even makin' him let me call on her."

They were coming up on Stagline's gate. To change the subject Frank said, "Why not get your blankets and bed down here for the night?"

"I'm shy on blankets," Stiles said ruefully. "Hocked 'em last week for a meal."

"We'll get you some."

The bunkhouse was empty. Frank was faintly uneasy over this until he remembered that Harmon had left just at dark to ride down to the new pasture station below The Narrows with provisions for Yates and young Bob Aspen. He supposed that Walters, the driver who had brought the stage in tonight, was somewhere downtown and wouldn't be in until late. He found blankets and Stiles made up an empty bunk.

Frank told his new man, "Turn in if you want. I've got work to do in the office." When he left the bunkhouse, Stiles was taking off his boots, too engrossed with his dark thoughts even to say good night.

After lighting the office lamp, Frank went around the desk to take the chair behind it. His thigh brushed against the weight of his holstered gun that hung from the chair back, reminding him of his reason for not having worn it tonight. As he cinched it about his waist again, his flat-planed face took on a faint smile at thought of the fight at the Paradise. The knuckles of his left hand still ached from the punch he'd thrown at Cliff Havens' jaw. He could still feel the hot savage surge of elation that had run through him as he and Stiles had made the doors. He hadn't wanted this thing to break into the open so soon, but now that Phenego had shown his hand he had no regrets.

Tonight he wanted to finish work on the big thick metal-bound accounts book that still lacked a few entries to show Stagline's financial standing. Tomorrow he intended taking the ledger with him on some calls on customers; he would try and show them in plain figures the necessity for their continued patronage, for common sense told him that none of Paul Le Soeur's old customers would want to see his daughter fail through the withdrawing of their business. He also wanted to see

Osgood about the possibility of adding new customers.

Less than five minutes after he had begun work on the ledger the lamp's flame started smoking and burning out. He shook the lamp and found it dry of oil. He looked through the office for more coal oil but couldn't find any. Then he remembered the table and the lamp in the bunkhouse and decided to go over there to finish his work.

He locked the office door. Crossing the darkened platform, he hefted the heavy ledger up under his left arm. His boot was groping for the platform's top step when a sudden shot exploded across the yard.

At the instant the sound came, the ledger was struck a hard blow that pounded it against his ribs. There was a stab of pain low along his chest as he staggered back under the bullet's impact. He lost his hold on the ledger, and it fell at the exact moment he wheeled to face a winking pin point of light he had caught at the limit of his vision. And as he wheeled toward the open-fronted shed opposite, his right hand was blurring his .38 up from hip.

His arm jumped to the whip of his gun's explosion as the weapon across there, on the roof of the shed, blossomed powder flame once more. The breath of that second bullet touched his cheek. He knew he'd missed his first shot and lifted the Colt to eye level, sure of his target now. He let his thumb slip from the gun's hammer and threw two thought-quick shots across there. On the heel of the last he saw a vague break in the shadowed flat line of the shed's roof. A hoarse choked cry came across to him. Then a man's cartwheeling shape fell groundward from the roof. A heavy thud marked the end of its fall.

He heard the bunkhouse door slam back against the wall and Stiles called sharply, "Justice!"

"Careful!" Frank answered. "He's across by that first shed." Holding his left elbow tight to his side against the moistness he could feel there, he jumped down from the platform and crouched in front of it, gun held ready.

But the dark blob lying on the ground across the yard didn't move. He heard Stiles running across from the bunkhouse to the end shed and came to his feet and

91

started over past the gate. By the time he stood looking down at the sprawled face-down body by the shed, Stiles was approaching, a gun in his hand.

Stiles knelt to turn the man over. He was dead. Stiles swore softly, saying, "That's shootin', brother!" and let the body roll back again.

"Know him?" Frank queried.

Stiles shook his head. "Never saw him before." Glancing up, he saw the dark stain along Frank's shirt and came abruptly erect. "You're bleedin'!"

"Forget it!" Frank told him. "We stay here on the chance he wasn't alone."

"I stay. You get inside and have a look at your side. Can you make it alone?" There was real concern in the new crewman's voice.

Stiles was insistent, so Frank left him and headed for the bunkhouse. He swung aside toward the platform and groped in the darkness there until he found the ledger. He took it with him. Before he lit the bunkhouse lamp he hung blankets over the two windows.

As he was taking off his shirt, he looked down at the ledger lying on the table. The cloth covering of its metal binder was torn and jagged ends of metal curled from an uneven hole. His own blood stained the edges of the cloth. Turning the ledger over, he found a neat hole on the other side marking the place the bullet had entered. He didn't need the searing pain along his ribs to tell him that the bushwhacker had laid his sights in line with his heart.

The bullet had torn his flesh and the bleeding was bad. But a rib had turned the slug and it now lay imbedded under the bruise that purpled his skin. He went to the stove and threw wood on the near-dead coals of the fire. He took down a shallow pan from a hook on the wall behind the stove and ladled a dipperful of water into it. Then, when the fire was roaring, he opened the stove's draft door and held the long blade of his clasp knife over the glowing coals.

When Ned Stiles came into the room twenty minutes later, Frank was sitting in one of the bunks, his lean face so completely drained of color that Stiles came quickly over to him, asking urgently, "You all right?"

Frank nodded. Then Stiles noticed other things: the bandage around Frank's chest, the torn ledger on the table, the flattened slug that lay near it, and the bottle of iodine on the chair. He felt the stifling warmth of the room and saw the pan of boiling water on the stove and the torn pieces of a clean flour sack hanging over the edge of the wood box. He understood then what had happened and the glance he turned on Frank was a blend of awe and admiration.

He said evenly, "There ought to be somethin' to help that," and searched in the cupboard behind the stove, then the bunks. In the pocket of a heavy jacket lying in one of the unused bunks he found a near-empty pint bottle of whisky. He brought it across to Frank, drawling, "You need this worse than I do."

The liquor brought a little of Frank's color back. When he'd taken his second pull at the bottle, he asked, "Anyone been around?"

Stiles shook his head.

"We'll take him out and bury him," Frank said. "In a place where they won't find him. Someone just might get curious enough to come around askin' a few questions if we keep this to ourselves."

Stiles said soberly, "You can count on me."

"I should have warned you about something like this before you took the job. You're free to quit any time you want."

The redhead's face took on a momentary flush of anger. Then he grinned good-naturedly. "You must be off your feed, Justice. Ain't I made it plain how I feel about Phenego and Brice?"

Frank smiled and began pulling on his shirt. "Then get a shovel and we'll get busy."

"No you don't! I'll do it alone. There ought to be a handy cut-bank up the canyon to cave in on that coyote bait. I won't need a shovel."

"I'll come along and watch." As he stood erect, Frank nodded to the table. "Better hide those things. I don't want Harmon or Walters to walk in on 'em."

Stiles saw there was no use arguing. Twenty minutes later they left the yard, the dead man's loose weight rolled in a tarp and tied on behind the cantle of Ned Stiles' saddle. It was nearly two in the morning before they rode back into the yard again. Harmon and Walters were in their bunks, Harmon snoring soundly.

VII

FOUR MILES north of Goldrock the climbing canyon widened to enclose a saucerlike valley close to half a mile wide. Thin jackpine timber ran down the slopes of this depression to the twisting bed of the canyon and there, along the trickle of a spring-fed stream, stood a cluster of weathered buildings that had once been the beginnings of a cow town.

A blacksmith by the name of James had put up the first building, thinking to make a living on the hill ranches dotting the open meadows higher toward the peaks. A saloon, eight or ten stores, and a motley assortment of lesser businesses had built around his shop before the boom at Goldrock had drained the uplands of its settlers. Jamestown, better known as Jimtown, had now been forgotten by all but a few; those few represented the dregs of Goldrock's seething life: down-and-outers, saddle bums, a few outlaws whose night riding had made living within the bounds of Phenego's easy law too precarious. By day Jimtown looked deserted, loose boards on

96

its two false-fronted buildings banging in the wind, its weed-grown street swirling with dust. At night it seemed empty, too, except that occasionally a pony or two would be tied to the rotting tie rails before the saloon. On those nights slivers of feeble light would be showing through the cracks of the saloon's boarded-up windows, and one or two of the better-preserved but ruined buildings might give out furtive sounds of occupancy.

East, across the valley from Jimtown, under the canyon's high boulder-strewn rim, were the shaft houses of five mines. Two of these were the biggest producers in the Goldrock district, the Combination and the Pearl, their muck dumps grayly marring the green belt of timber that footed the rim. A year and a half ago a geologist brought in by an Eastern outfit had strayed up here and noticed the volcanic formation of the rock up near the rim. He had staked out the Combination claim for his employers. Within three months all the ground below the rim had been taken up and machinery was coming in. Now the procession of ore wagons that drove between these mines and the reducing mill below Goldrock ignored the old

97

trail that led through Jimtown and used a new road.

Mike Shannon, superintendent of the Combination, had had a heavy day. His assayer was running a test on what looked like rich ore brought up from the newly extended stope on the fourth level. Now, at three o'clock, he was getting ready his report to mail to the home office in the morning. He was a short, solid, red-faced Irishman with a bald head. Detail work such as this report irritated him.

He was therefore gruff with his clerk, who came into the office to say that a man wanted to see him. "Get rid of him," Shannon snapped. "I've got more'n enough to—"

He stopped speaking as a tall wide-hatted figure stepped into the doorway behind his clerk. He scowled, said, "No time today. See me tomorrow."

Frank Justice reached out a hand to keep the clerk from closing the door on him, saying, "Tomorrow won't do, Shannon."

"Why won't it?" The superintendent's tone was curt, his look suspicious.

Frank stepped past the clerk and on into the room. Shannon swung around on his high stool from the wall desk. "See here!"

"This won't take long," Frank interrupted. "I'm after your bullion-freighting business, Mr. Shannon. I can take only a certain amount and I thought you'd like to get in on it."

"Then you've come a long way for nothin', me lad." Shannon couldn't keep up the pretense of anger, for he liked this man's directness. "We're doin' business with Mountain Stages. They do a good job and there's no complaint." He swung around to his desk again. "Now if you'll . . ."

He paused as Frank smiled. "What's so funny?"

"I was just thinkin' how riled you'll be when you hear about it."

"About what?"

"The fifteen-dollar rate I'm offerin' your neighbors down the line."

Shannon's brows lifted quizzically. "Fifteen? You can't do it for that. I pay twenty now and that's low. Mountain is crowin' about a raise after the next trip."

Frank shrugged and turned to the door. "Suit yourself, Shannon. I'm in a hurry. So long."

"Hold on!" Shannon came down off the stool and went to the door to close it after motioning his clerk out. When he turned to face Frank again, he waved to a chair. "Sit down."

Frank took out his watch, looked at it, and shook his head. "Can't. I've got these other calls to make."

"Take it easy," Shannon said. He eyed Frank with suddenly renewed interest. "Didn't I see you at the Paradise last night?"

"I was there."

Shannon's smile came slowly. "I'll say you were. When you've got the time, I'd like you to show me that uppercut you used on Havens. First time he was ever knocked off his feet, I hear. So you're the gent that's taken over Le Soeur's outfit?" He considered Frank levelly a moment, after which he gave a deliberate shake of the head. "You can't do it, Justice. Not for fifteen dollars on the thousand."

"Does anyone tell you how to run your business, Shannon? I can make a profit if you and the rest will sign six-month contracts to keep Mountain from under-bidding me."

"We don't give contracts for freighting bullion. Suppose you lose a shipment?"

"I'd put up a bond."

"You couldn't put up one to cover a big loss. Sometimes we ship upwards of fifty thousand at a time."

"Mountain couldn't cover a loss like that either. What bond do they give?"

"Five thousand at interest."

"Wouldn't my five thousand be as good?" Frank drawled. "You're getting a quarter cut in the rate. That would amount to something over a six-month period."

Shannon nodded. "It would. But where would you lay hands on the money to put up bond? It's bein' talked around that your outfit is cuttin' it pretty thin these days."

Frank walked past Shannon to the desk. He tore a piece of paper from a tablet, reached for a pen, and began writing. When he'd finished, he handed the paper across.

Shannon eyed it for a moment. "What good is an option on a half interest in your outfit going to do me?"

"I've named a purchase price there. A dollar."

"I still don't see it, Justice."

"Yesterday we turned down an offer of ten thousand for Stagline. Matt Phenego made the offer, which is about half what the outfit's worth. If you ever have to take up that bond you'll be getting close to ten thousand dollars instead of the five you'd get from Mountain to cover any loss. So I'm doubling their bond and giving you a quarter cut in rates. In return you give me half a year's contract to give me time to come out ahead on all the new equipment we're bringin' in to take care of new business." He paused to let that sink in. Then, "If you're not interested, say so and I'll be on my way."

Shannon deliberated a long moment. Then he went across and sat on his high stool, picking up the pen as he said, "You'll have to deposit your deed with our bank in Alkali. How do you want the contract worded?"

A long slow sigh escaped Frank's wide chest. Although he hadn't showed it, his nerves were taut and his palms moist with perspiration. Here was the opening wedge to break apart the day's earlier disappointments. This morning his call at Wells-Fargo had netted him a loss; Chapin, the express manager, had informed him that hereafter he would split his business between Mountain and Stagline, where heretofore he had given it all to Le Soeur.

102

On leaving Chapin he'd stopped in to see Osgood and learned that the Placer Miners Association had that morning canceled their agreement with Stagline in favor of Phenego's line. Brice was responsible for that, having offered the association a reduction in rates. Brice's maneuver had given Frank the idea of tackling Mountain's customers. He had picked the biggest first, the Combination.

Less than ten minutes later Shannon was handing across the contract. "That'll do until I have time to stop in and have Sam Osgood draw up a better one. Tell Osgood we'll want an assignment. That means you'll have to turn over the deed to the bank. We ship on Friday, day after tomorrow."

He walked through the front office and out the door with Frank. The chugging of the winch engine in the shaft house sent echoes running along the rim towering high overhead. A dump car rolled out the rails to the end of the conical muck heap.

Frank pointed obliquely downward to the rusting sheet-iron roof of a shaft house lower along the slope than this one and farther up the valley. "What happened there?"

"The Oriole?" Shannon shrugged. "Piece o' bad luck. There's a wide fault at the foot of the rim. It's full of rubble that must have washed into it a few centuries ago. We struck it close to our lower line and had to abandon work there. But the Oriole got it on two sides and we had to shut down early last summer. Now it's filling with water. I'd sure hate to have held any of their stock."

Frank remembered what Ned Stiles had said last night about Helen Moreford's brother working as watchman on an abandoned mine up here. Then Shannon was saying, "Good luck, lad. And if it'll help you any, you can show that contract to Belden and the others down the way."

Shannon's contract was all Frank needed to get the bullion-freighting business of the four other mines along the rim. The managers of the Nugget and the Dolly Madison, smaller than their neighbors, were impressed by Shannon's action. But Belden, of the Pearl, was cautious and deliberate in agreeing. He was the last man Frank saw, and by that time the dusk was thick enough to make a lamp necessary in the Pearl's office shack.

When Frank had explained the nature

of his business and mentioned Shannon's contract, Belden's first word was, "You'll have to put up a bond."

Frank had been expecting this and wanting to avoid it as he had the three other smaller outfits he'd seen since leaving Shannon. So he tried to hedge, saying, "You're getting a cut in rates."

"That may be; but you're new here, Justice. Mountain put up a bond and so will you. It ain't that I don't trust you, but the owners would give me hell for goin' whole hog with a stranger. I'll have to have the bond."

Frank thought at first he'd have to lose Belden's business. The Pearl's account represented a sizable amount, too much to be hastily put aside. About to give up, he had a thought that made him abruptly give in to Belden. When he left the mine, he had a fifth contract in his pocket. But there was a condition attached. He'd given Belden his promise that Belle Le Soeur would sign over her half interest in Stagline as the required bond.

Heading down the trail toward Goldrock as the last feeble light of day waned on the peaks, he tried to believe that Belle Le Soeur would give her consent to this gamble. And it was a gamble, he told himself. The combined shipments of these five mines on Friday would total more than sixty thousand dollars in bullion. If anything happened . . .

But he put that thought from his mind and chose to think, instead, of the nine-hundred-dollar fee the mines would be paying. With that money he could afford to hire more men; perhaps add another uptrip to meet the afternoon train at Alkali, a trip Le Soeur had abandoned because he feared trouble with Mountain, according to Burkitt.

He rode with his left boot out of the stirrup, favoring his left side. The stiff draw of his chest wound was a reminder of the chance he was taking. Last night he and Ned Stiles had buried the dead man three miles back from the canyon's west rim. The fact that no one had shown curiosity over the shots wasn't surprising, for Goldrock had become hardened to the sound of guns. But he had been counting on Phenego trying to find out what had happened to his hired killer, sure that Phenego had sent the man after him. Faunce, at least, should have made some inquiry. But neither Faunce nor anyone else had appeared at the yard this morning and there was no talk on the street that could possibly be associated with what had happened last night. The situation puzzled Frank and made him wonder how deep a game Phenego was playing.

And now that he could consider the thing logically, he saw the error of risking Belle Le Soeur's small inheritance in a gamble like this. His enthusiasm had carried him too far. He would regret having to back out of his agreement with Belden, but he decided finally he'd have to.

He had a few rare moments on that ride down the canyon when there was no sound but the muffled stomp of his walking pony and the creak of saddle leather, when the rumble of the ore wagons was muted into nothingness by the distance and he had the nerve-relaxing feeling that he was utterly alone. He felt a strong nostalgia for the solitary life he had just left behind in quitting his ranch; this brief interval when he rode beneath a star-studded sky, listening to the whisper of the wind through the pines that flanked the trail, was a tonic he found he'd badly needed to ease the strain of the last two days.

His enjoyment of the moment was

abruptly ended as his pony lifted its head, ears erect. Then out of the shadows of the timber nearly sixty feet away to his left he saw a rider moving slowly in toward him. His long body stiffened and his hand fell to his thigh.

At that precise instant a voice called sharply from the other side of the trail, close, "Stay set, Justice!"

His glance came around to see a second rider, much closer, approaching, a rider who cradled a Winchester across the horn of his saddle. And now the one to his left had halted. Another materialized out of the trees over there.

Frank checked the immediate urge to ram spurs to his pony's flanks. He slowly lifted his hands. The rider with the Winchester came closer—close enough for Frank to recognize him as the first Paradise man he had dropped with that lucky punch at the bar last night, Cliff Havens.

"Keep 'em lifted!" Havens drawled as he put his horse close alongside. "This is just a friendly gatherin'. We were thinkin' you'd like a second try at what you started last night."

He moved his reins to his rifle hand, the rifle downmuzzled on the far side of his pony's neck now, and reached out with his left hand for Frank's gun as he put his weight in his near stirrup.

Frank sensed in that split second that Havens was off balance, also that the other pair were not yet close enough to catch any detail of movement. And he knew that, once disarmed, he would get the beating they had failed to give him last night.

He brought his right arm down in a palm-edge chop at Havens' outstretched hand. He caught the man sharply on the wrist in a numbing blow. His fist closed about that wrist and jerked Havens sideways out of the saddle. And his reaching left hand caught the uparching rifle barrel and twisted it from Havens grasp as the man cried out.

His pony shied and he threw himself out of the saddle, dragging Havens aground. Havens fell full-length and Frank let his weight go down onto him, hitting him in the chest with his knees as he caught the dragging reins of Havens' pony. The man's breath left his lungs in a choked groan as a shot exploded across the stillness. Kneeling on the stunned man, Frank turned and lifted the rifle to his shoulder. He laid his sights quickly on the nearest rider and squeezed the trigger. His bullet drove Havens' companion from the saddle in an ungainly dive as his horse reared.

He wheeled erect and in behind Havens' pony, drawling, "Tell 'em to be good!"

Coughing, gasping for breath, Havens rolled onto an elbow and called hoarsely, "He's got us, Roerick! Lay off!"

The man who had been unsaddled by Frank's bullet was on his feet now, trying to catch his pony's swinging reins with one hand while his other arm hung loosely at his side. His companion, in the act of reaching down for his gun, hesitated at Havens' call and slowly raised his hands.

VIII

Jim Faunce saw Stiles coming along the crowded walk toward him and immediately turned into a lighted store doorway, hoping to avoid the meeting. But as Stiles came even with the doorway he broke from his saunter and swung suddenly around, confronting the marshal. His small body was slightly cocked at the waist and his right hand hung significantly close to the handle of his gun.

Stiles drawled tauntingly, "Go ahead! Make your play!"

Faunce's thin face went sallow before the redhead's blunt invitation. He was careful to keep his hand clear of his low-slung holster as he said, "No one's goin' to bother you, Stiles. Ease off!"

Ned Stiles had the galling memory of the past two weeks to whet his anger, and his scorn of this man. In those two weeks he'd tried without success to get the marshal to collect Phenego's bad debt, finally knowing where Faunce's allegiance lay. Bred to a loathing of dishonesty, he had at first looked on Faunce as a thoroughly dangerous man; in the end he knew him to be nothing but a weakling, a petty understrapper. Once convinced of that, he had been open in his dislike of the lawman.

He said, "Where's your guts, Faunce? You shied in there when you saw me comin'. All right, back it up!"

A few men passing along the walk had stopped now, recognizing the marshal and sensing that something out of the ordinary was going on here. As Stiles now spoke they moved out of line with him and retreated a step or two but still stayed to watch.

"Go along, Stiles," Faunce breathed almost inaudibly, cold fury in his eyes.

"Supposin' you move first," Stiles drawled. "Think I'd trust you at my back?"

There was a moment in which Stiles thought Faunce was going to break under that insult. But at length the marshal came down off the doorstep and went on up the walk. He didn't even turn as a spectator who had witnessed the encounter guffawed loudly at his back.

Faunce was boiling under the humiliation Stiles had thrust upon him as he came even with Paradise's swing doors. About to turn in there for a badly needed drink, he suddenly changed his mind. He hated the saloon and all it stood for; he hated Phenego for what Phenego had done to him. For the first time in his life he was seeing himself for what he was and there was a hot shame in him. Looking back into his past, he couldn't put his finger on the exact moment he had thrust behind him the ethics of a solid upbringing and become a dishonest man. He supposed it was the day he'd had to leave his home country, the day a neighbor caught him heating a running iron in a fire with a roped unbranded calf lying close by. The calf had belonged to the neighbor. That seemed long ago, for much had happened since. There had been more rustling, cards, a few women; he'd even looked across his sights at a man's back. He had excused all this in thinking he was crowded into it by circumstances. Now he knew that the real reason lay in a weakness deep within him and this truth, one he could no longer evade, filled him with a strong self-loathing.

He was past the Paradise when he heard the shouts on the street and looked out there and saw Frank Justice turning in toward the saloon's hitch rail. Justice had a rifle laid across the swell of his saddle. Before him three men rode single file. Cliff Havens, hatless, pale, and sitting hunched over in the saddle as though favoring a broken rib, led the way, followed by Roerick and Ed Curran. There was blood on the shoulder of Roerick's coat and that arm was thrust into his shirt, which served as a sling. They dismounted at the rail in front of the Paradise, Roerick awkwardly and wincing as he came around. The crowd there slowly opened a lane to the swing doors.

Justice sat his pony a few feet out from

the rumps of those at the rail. Faunce saw him deliberately toss a rifle and three six-guns to the ground and heard his drawled, "Better luck next time, Havens."

Then he reined out and, his back to Havens and his men, started up the street.

The meaning behind this brief scene was clear to Faunce. He saw it as Phenego's second failure at getting the best of Frank Justice. Then, because it was the way his mind worked, Faunce's hand fell to the butt of his Colt and he looked back over his shoulder to find himself within a step of the narrow passageway leading between the saloon and the neighboring building. A wagon moved from between him and Justice and he had a nice chance to draw, target Justice, and shoot. But in the act of lifting his weapon from leather he paused, held by the same feeling that had been with him since meeting Stiles. By killing Justice he would be doing Phenego a favor. If Phenego was here by his side he would undoubtedly order him to shoot. But the new-found rebellion in him stiffened. Damned if he'd do Phenego's chores for the pay he was getting, for any pay!

When Justice had ridden on out of

range, Jim Faunce breathed a gusty prolonged sigh. He felt strangely better than
a moment ago. This act somehow bolstered a nearly lost pride, made him feel
cleaner. He dismissed his growing dislike
of Matt Phenego as the reason he hadn't
drawn on Justice and began thinking that
it was because he hadn't wanted to take
unfair advantage of a man. When he went
on down the walk his shoulders had lifted
from their habitual slouch and he held his
head higher. Then, about to turn in at
a saloon up the street, he went on past
its door and on to a restaurant. Tonight
he didn't feel the need of liquor to ease
an uncomfortable mind.

For the first time in many months Jim
Faunce took a look at himself and wasn't
ashamed.

Turning out from the saloon tie rail into
the traffic of the street, Frank's back
crawled at the threat behind him. Havens'
and Roerick's and the third houseman's
guns lay out beyond the gutter, within two
strides of them. But Frank was crowding
his luck, playing the hunch that they
wouldn't dare make a move against him
in front of the crowd, even in the face

of their humiliation. He didn't look back and his complete ignoring of them was an openly scornful gesture that brought laughs from the watchers, along with a few ribald shouts of derision directed at Havens and his men.

When he had ridden out of range, he felt a slow letdown. Only now that it was over did he realize how tight-drawn his nerves had been these past twenty minutes, since pulling Havens from the saddle on the Jimtown trail. His mouth was parched and his hand wanted to tremble.

He suspected that the three Paradise men had been working off their own personal grudge in stopping him and hadn't acted on Phenego's orders. He'd been lucky, damned lucky, to be able to turn their viciousness back upon them. It was typical of him to have brought them in and made them eat crow publicly. The word would get to Phenego even if they didn't report to him. Nothing would strike home to Phenego quite as strongly as having his own tactics used against him.

By the time he was within sight of the glow of Stagline's platform lantern lighting the gate he was himself once more, the aftereffects of his encounter drained out of him. He walked his pony in through the gate feeling all at once hungry and tired. He hadn't had much sleep last night and his side still ached a little, but the wound was healing fast. He wondered what Stiles would have to report on inquiries after the dead bushwhacker.

"Frank!"

As his glance swung over to the platform, he had already recognized the voice that hailed him as Belle Le Soeur's. She was coming out from the office door, a slender and graceful shape in the lantern's light as she crossed the platform to meet him.

He caught strong alarm in her face and her eyes were wide. "There's been trouble, a stage holdup!" she told him, her voice tense. "Fred Cash was hurt. He's in the bunkhouse with Harmon and that new man."

"How bad is he?" Frank asked, lifting the reins.

"I don't know. I've been here in the office talking to the passengers. Send me word as soon as you can."

As he vaulted from the saddle in front of the bunkhouse, he saw the mud wagon back by the corrals, two teams in harness where there should have been three. He took the bunkhouse steps in a single stride and swung in the door.

Fred Cash sat by the table at the long room's center. His right trouser leg had been slit halfway to the hip and his stringy white-fleshed thigh lay bare. The glare of the unshaded lamp overhead made the oldster's sweat-moist face glisten. They all looked at Frank as he came in, Cash with relief, Harmon and Stiles frowning at the interruption. Stiles knelt behind the chair, holding the oldster's arms tight behind the chair back. Harmon was stooped over, a wadded iodine-soaked rag in his hand, about to press it against an ugly long wound on the top of Cash's thigh.

Cash bawled, "Stop 'em, boss! It's nothin' but a scratch! It'll get well without—" There came his swift intake of breath as Harmon applied the iodine. His teeth clenched and his face reddened. He held his breath a long moment, then exhaled with a relieved salty oath. Ned let his arms go and he grinned up at Harmon, his face pain-etched, saying, "Not so bad."

A bullet had creased a deep channel in the flesh at the top of Cash's thigh. It was painful but not serious. As Harmon applied a bandage, the oldster told his story. "Three jaspers with their faces covered stopped us right after dark, above The Narrows. Shot out my lanterns the first thing. I was loco enough to reach for the scatter gun behind the seat. If I hadn't been leaning back, this slug would have cut me in two. I clawed the air and stayed that way while they made the passengers get out and went through their pockets. One of the passengers tried to hide his wallet and had a gun barrel bent over his skull. Before they left they shot two of my horses so as to make good their getaway." He shook his head ruefully. "And I was all set to lower Burkitt's time for the uptrip! Would of, too, if they hadn't stopped me."

"How did the passengers take it?" Frank asked.

Cash shrugged. "Ask Belle. She took care of 'em."

Ned put in, "They lost a hundred and forty dollars between 'em. One, a dry-goods drummer, threatened to sue. But the Le Soeur girl talked him out of it. She paid back half the money they lost. They'll get the other half a week from now, providin' no news of the holdup has leaked out into the town." His freckled face took on a smile. "It was all her idea. She's got a head on her shoulders."

Harmon asked, "What about a driver in the mornin', Justice? Fred's going to be laid up a couple days."

Frank hadn't thought of that. He saw now that the wounding of Fred Cash had put them in a tight spot. Walters, the only other driver, was in Alkali, having taken the morning stage down.

He was about to say he'd drive, himself, when Ned drawled, "What's the matter with me?"

"Ever handled a three-team hitch, Ned?" Harmon asked.

"Plenty of times."

Frank was the only one able to see Ned's face as he gave his answer, and he knew that the redheaded 'puncher was lying. But he didn't call him on it, saying, to change the subject, "Get into your blankets, Cash. We'll have some food sent up. Keep off your feet a couple days." He nodded to Ned as he turned to the door. "We'd better get those horses into the corral."

Outside, the door closed behind them, he asked Ned, "Think you can make the drive?"

"I can try."

"We might be able to find a driver in town."

Ned shook his head. "Not a chance. We were talkin' about it before you came in. Drivers are scarce."

Frank was silent a moment, sober under the news Ned had given him. Then he asked, "Anyone drop in today to find out about our friend we buried last night?"

"No. And I was here the whole day. What do you reckon Phenego's play is?"

"I wish I knew," Frank admitted honestly, for it wasn't like Phenego to send a man on an errand like the bushwhacker's and then not be curious when he mysteriously disappeared.

Ned nodded toward the shack by the gate. "You'd better get up there and tell the girl about Cash. She was plenty worried about him. I'll turn these horses in." He gave Frank a long, level look, not immediately turning away. Then he asked bluntly, "You goin' to let this go by without an answer, Frank?"

"Let what go by?"

"Phenego stoppin' one of our stages and shootin' up our driver. There's three of us, you and Harmon and me. We could go tear up Phenego's joint."

"Then we would be in a spot." Frank shook his head. "No, we'll let it ride for now. Don't worry; we'll get our chance at Phenego."

"Wish I was as sure of that as you are," Ned said, starting over to the mud wagon.

Belle was waiting in the office. As Frank came in off the platform she asked quickly, "How is he?"

"Not bad," Frank told her. "He'll be around in a day or so. But he won't be able to work."

"That means we need a driver."

"Stiles can manage for one trip." As he saw the concern fade from her face, he wished he could believe what he had told her. Then his own worry eased, for she was regarding him in a half-smiling way that spoke of a change from her antagonism of yesterday during the interview with Osgood. Only then did he remember her calling him by name as he rode into the yard. That, and her friendliness now, puzzled him. He said, "You can probably stand a piece of good news. I was up in Jimtown this afternoon." He drew the contracts from his pocket and laid them on the desk before her. "Have a look."

She opened one to read it, gave him a startled glance, and went on to the rest. She caught her breath when she saw Shannon's name. "This is . . . Is it true? The Combination, the Pearl?"

He had forgotten Belden's contract and now took it from the others. "All but Belden's. We'll have to skip him for now."

She was quick to sense the abrupt change in his manner and it in turn sobered her. "What was the trouble?"

"He wanted a heavy bond. We can't give it."

She frowned. "Didn't the Combination ask for one?"

He nodded. "I signed over my share of the outfit to meet it. Shannon was satisfied. Belden had drawn up the contract before we got down to cases." He hoped his twisting of the circumstances would deceive her.

It didn't. She said, "There's my share. Why didn't you offer him that?" He was surprised and showed it. She saw the color mount to his face and quick understanding came to her, for she breathed, "You did think of it!"

He said, "Sure, at first. Then afterward I . . ."

As he paused, a warm smile tilted up the corners of her lips. "You were afraid for me, weren't you?"

He said flatly, "Phenego's got playful ways. He'll get rough with us."

"He tried it last night, didn't he?" She laughed softly at his momentary confusion before reminding him of the fight at the Paradise. "You could probably do it alone, Frank. But it's selfish of me to let you down." She stood up from her chair behind the desk. "We'll make good Belden's contract. We're together in this. And now, if you're not too busy to spare me an hour, we could talk all this over down in the dining room at the hotel. I've been here waiting to see you since four and it's given me an appetite."

By the time she took his arm as they were going down the walk, Frank Justice was too confused to be aware of anything but the sudden change in his luck—of that and of Belle Le Soeur's nearness, the light touch of her hand on his arm, and the friendly lilt of her voice as their talk sealed a new and strange bond of understanding between them.

IX

Eᴅ Bʀɪᴄᴇ watched the big Concord being unloaded in the glare of the lanterns along Mountain's runway, satisfied when his count of the passengers totaled eleven. Then he forgot that as he recognized the driver, Hoff, the man who had two nights ago rammed Stagline's mud wagon on the street out front and caused the accident.

Even before the accident, he had known Hoff was a thin sour-faced man who was the most capable of Mountain's crew but also clearly aware of his importance. Hoff's working schedule called for his taking a stage down to Baker's Crossing station each morning and waiting there until early afternoon to relieve the driver on the inbound; he worked a lighter day than any of the other drivers, but to make up for this the road up the canyon was the hardest part of the long Alkali run. Even though the man was thoroughly capable, a strong irritation was Brice's invariable reaction at sight of him. And seeing that Hoff now made no move to climb down from his seat and help the crew unload made that feeling stronger than ever.

He nodded curtly as Hoff wheeled the big coach past him and on into the yard, the three teams of Morgans stepping out smartly. Hoff made a wide fast swing over toward the sheds and close in to their awnings before turning sharply out in front of the wagon shed. Hoff had started that outward swing when the coach suddenly jolted to an abrupt stop. There came the sound of splintering wood and the big Concord swayed sharply in toward the awning, rocking on its thorough braces. Then Hoff was shouting an oath and trying to back his nervous teams, using the whip.

Brice ran over there in time to see the Concord's front wheel hub wedged against an awning pillar. At that moment Hoff backed clear and the wheel's sprung spokes gave way and the coach settled down onto the axle with a grating jar.

Hoff climbed down cursing obscenely, unaware of Brice.

At Brice's sharp-edged, "Nice work, Hoff!" he swung around, his face set belligerently.

"It was that jugheaded on-leader!" Hoff

flared. "I told 'em not to put him in harness."

"Maybe you'd like a stretch on the hay wagons," Brice drawled.

The driver's face took on a sultry sneer. He threw his reins to the ground and tossed his whip in through the coach's open window in an eloquent gesture of disgust.

The damage had resulted plainly from Hoff's carelessness. Perhaps he was right in blaming one of his horses. Brice would have let it go with any of the other drivers, but he took a grim pleasure in riding Hoff.

"What's the matter, drunk?" he said in biting sarcasm.

"Sure," Hoff drawled, "drunk as a goat!"

The man's insolence snapped a thread of Brice's reasoning. He reached out suddenly and took a hold on Hoff's coat and drew the man toward him in an off-balanced lurch.

"Shoot off your mouth at me again and you're through, Hoff!"

"Who's shootin' his mouth off?" Hoff swung an arm to knock Brice's hand down as he snarled the words.

Brice's free hand fisted and struck a hard

sideward blow that caught the driver full on the cheek and rocked his head around. As quick as the flicking tongue of a snake, Brice's grip on his driver's coat loosed and tilted Hoff's head around again in a hard openhanded slap. Hoff reeled backward against the front of the shed in under the awning. His wide Stetson lay on the ground, his stringy gray hair falling down over one eye. A line of blood ran down from one corner of his thin lips and the gleam of pure hate was in his eyes.

From the inner mouth of the runway sounded a hushed undertone of voices. Looking over there, Brice saw that four men of the crew had witnessed this ungovernable show of temper in him and he was all at once uncomfortable before their scrutiny.

But now that he'd started this he had to finish it. He snapped, "Go to the office and get your pay, Hoff. You're through!"

"Keep your damned pay!" Hoff muttered.

Wiping his bleeding mouth with the back of his hand, he reached down for his Stetson, clamped it on his head, and strode out the runway and out of sight onto the street.

Brice called to his crewmen, "Get over here and clean up this mess!"

Hal Closson, one of the three men Brice had yesterday brought with him from Stagline at a sizable increase in pay, helped unhitch the teams and jack up the Concord's axle while a new wheel was put on. Then, past quitting time, Closson left the yard and turned up the street. He found Harmon and Fred Cash and Ned Stiles in Stagline's bunkhouse and called Harmon outside and told him what had happened.

The change that came over Hoff once he was well down the walk beyond Mountain's gateway would have interested Brice. The expression of dark anger left his face and was replaced by a tight-lipped smile. That smile stayed with him all the way to the Paradise, where he turned in and made his way back to Matt Phenego's office. Once inside the office, the smile even broadened.

Phenego read something into Hoff's expression that made him say, "It must've worked."

"Like a charm, boss, like a charm!"

"Any witnesses?"

"Plenty. Closson and three others saw it."

"What happened to your face?"

"Brice swung on me after I busted a front wheel of the coach."

Phenego's glance was tinged with respect. "Good." He leaned back in his chair to take a roll of bills from a pocket. He thumbed half a dozen from the roll and held them out to Hoff. "This'll help heal you up, Hoff. Don't spend it tonight. Hit the saloons, but go easy on the drinks. Before morning you'll have another job."

"You're a damn' sight surer than I am about that."

"Take my word for it. Justice will see you before the night's over."

Ned Stiles came up to the table as Frank and Belle were finishing their meal. He was plainly embarrassed as he said, "Mind if I speak to you for a minute, Frank?"

It was at once clear that Ned had something important on his mind and didn't want to mention it in front of the girl. "Go ahead," Frank said. "Let's have it."

"It's about a driver. Brice had a run-in with one of his men tonight, gent by the

130

name of Hoff. Beat him up and fired him. Hoff didn't even wait for his pay."

Frank placed Hoff as the driver of the Concord that had caused the accident the night of his arrival. "Where'd you hear about this?" he asked.

"Closson, a friend of Harmon's."

Frank looked at Belle. She said, "You can trust Closson's word. He left us only because he was offered more money."

"It could have been framed." Frank looked up at Ned.

Stiles slowly gave a shake of his head. "Not the way Closson told it. Brice lost his head. Him and Hoff have had it in for each other ever since Brice went with the outfit. It seems Hoff thought Phenego should have given him Brice's job."

Belle understood the direction in which Frank's thoughts were heading. "We could use a good man," she said. "And I can go home alone if you want to go try find Hoff."

"Not a chance," Ned put in with a broad grin. "I'm sort of out of practice, but I'd enjoy the walk, ma'am."

Frank caught Belle's nod and reached for his hat. "Careful, Ned, she's the boss," he said as he left the table.

They saw him stop at the lobby door and pay the waiter.

Later, as she and Ned came out onto the street, Belle said, "You may not have to drive tomorrow after all."

"To tell the truth, ma'am, it'll be a relief not to," he said.

Four doors above the hotel they came abreast of Mountain's runway. Abruptly Belle had a rebellious impulse that made her say, "I'll stop in and see Ed Brice a moment. You needn't wait."

Ned was surprised but touched his hat and said, "Sure he'll be in?"

When she nodded he left her. Brice was in the back office. He scowled as the door opened, but when he saw Belle his expression changed to a smiling one and there was a warm welcome in his voice as he came across to her, saying, "Belle! This is a surprise!" He drew a chair out from the wall and placed it by the desk. "I never thought to see you here."

"Nor did I." She looked around the big well-furnished room as she took the chair. "You've come up in the world, Ed."

"It wasn't because I wanted to, Belle," he said, at once grave. This mention of their differences reminded her of the impulse that had brought her here. "Ed, our evening stage was stopped above The Narrows tonight. The passengers were robbed and beaten. Fred Cash was wounded."

Studying his obvious surprise, Belle knew at once that he hadn't known about the holdup. When he breathed "No!" she was sure of it.

She said, "Now we don't have a driver to make the run down in the morning."

He swallowed with difficulty, seeming at a loss for something to say; for he knew she had come here suspecting him. In the end he found words. "I didn't know about it, Belle. I'll give you my oath I didn't. But . . ."

"But what?" she asked when he hesitated.

"There's always Phenego," he told her. "I can't know what he'll do." He sat on the corner of the desk close to her, looking down at her with an expression that seemed to plead for her understanding. "I'm sorry it happened, Belle; sorry it had to be Fred Cash. If you'll agree, I'll loan you a driver until you find one."

"You needn't. Frank is out now trying to find the man you let go tonight."

"Hoff?" he queried sharply, then laughed without amusement. "He's welcome to him." His glance went sober. "Frank? You mean Justice?"

There was a faint but unmistakable accusation behind his words. She ignored it, a strong pride mounting in her as she said, "Yes, Frank Justice. Have you heard that he went to Jimtown this afternoon and came back with contracts to freight out the bullion of the mines up there?"

Afterward she couldn't explain the satisfaction she took in speaking so bluntly, in seeing the dark flush that rode into his face.

"Shannon and Belden too?" he asked in a flat voice.

She nodded. "And the others." She was all at once sorry to be the bearer of such news, but at the same time on the defensive. "You couldn't expect Frank to take it lying down, could you? You're after our business and we're after yours."

He stood up and went around the desk to take the chair behind it, picking up a pencil and turning it endwise between his fingers. She found it hard to meet his direct stare in the following silence. Presently a faint smile touched his face but not his eyes. "What bond did you put up?"

"Stagline," she answered readily, ignoring the antagonism that seemed to be building between them.

"You mean you're gambling the line against this scheme of Justice's?" He all at once sat straighter in the chair. "Don't do it, Belle! You'll lose everything. Have you signed over the deed yet?"

"No. But I intend to in the morning."

"Don't you know that Phenego intends to ruin you . . . to run Justice out of the country?" He was so intent that some of the color left his face. "And don't you know that I can't stop him?"

"You didn't want to stop him yesterday," she reminded him. "Wasn't there something about your coming back after me when we didn't have a wheel rolling?"

"Belle! I was sore—sore at Justice for hornin' in where he had no right to. All I've got is a job. Not a job to ruin you or anyone else but one to earn us a living, you and me together. Have you forgotten that?"

The outright misery that lay back of his words touched her. She reached out and put a hand on his. "I'm sorry, Ed. But

135

I've changed my mind on one thing. I don't intend to let the line go. I'm going to stay with it. Frank Justice needs my help. I'd be selfish and ungrateful if I didn't give it to him."

"Where does that put me, Belle?"

"Can't we get along, both of us? Isn't there enough business to go around?"

"There is if Phenego can be made to understand. But he can't, Belle."

She was all at once weary of the tangle their talk had become. She said, "Will you take me home, Ed?"

He knew that nothing he could say or do would change her. Yet he made one more attempt. "Suppose I come back with Stagline?"

"Could you? Would Frank let you? I don't know, Ed."

Once again the ease with which she spoke Justice's name galled him. He shrugged and got up from the desk and held the door open for her. They didn't have much to say on the way up the street and into the lane that led up the slope to her house. It was as though they were mere acquaintances instead of a woman and a man who had yesterday spoken of marriage.

X

FRANK TURNED in at the first saloon below the hotel, playing the hunch that Hoff would be drinking tonight after losing a good job. A brassy clamor filled the Rosebud, and the air was stale and blue with tobacco smoke. Frank sauntered the length of the crowded bar and in between the watchers at the gambling layouts. When he left the saloon he was sure that Hoff wasn't there.

He tried the Melodion and the Queen with as little success. He thought he saw Hoff in the Desert Flower, but it was another man. Then, pushing through the crowd in front of the Paradise, he spotted Hoff passing him in the opposite direction. He turned and followed and was presently taking a stool beside Hoff at the counter of a restaurant down the street. He ordered coffee and pie and decided to wait and see if Hoff spoke to him, for he wasn't yet sure that Hoff's quitting wasn't a frame-up of Brice's to put one of his men on his competitor's pay roll.

But Hoff seemed unaware of him and

had finished his cup of coffee and was turning to leave the place when Frank said, "Remember me, Hoff?"

The man's response was a wide smile and, "Ought to, hadn't I?" The smile was nervous and somehow didn't fit his face, which was thin and long and inclined to severity. Frank recognized in him the stringy toughness and the big calloused hands that spoke of long acquaintance with his profession.

"Hear you lost your job tonight," he said.

An expression of wicked anger momentarily crossed Hoff's face. "Yeah."

"Goin' back when Brice cools off?"

Hoff's negative move of the head was deliberate. "I'll starve first."

"Want to hire on with us?"

Hoff was remembering the coaching Phenego had given him. He was quick-witted enough to decide that he had the job now if he wanted it, also shrewd enough to know that the better he played his part now the more use he could be to Phenego later on. So he shrugged his bony shoulders and drawled, "I thought about takin' a few days off. Haven't been on a good bender in a coon's age."

"Save it till payday. I'm short a driver for the morning trip. You'd be doing me a favor."

"What's the pay?"

"What've you been gettin'?"

"Sixty a week. Ten apiece for extra trips."

"That's pretty steep, Hoff."

Again Hoff gave that shrug. "I'm worth it."

This man's cocksureness appealed to Frank. He wanted to hire Hoff. But he also wanted to be sure of something else first. He said, "I pay fifty. Right now there's no pay for overtime." He smiled meagerly. "The gang I've got want to get a few other things settled first."

"Meanin' this scrap with Mountain?" There was an edge of eagerness to Hoff's tone now. He hoped it was convincing.

"That's the general idea."

"Then maybe I can hold off on that bender." Hoff ran his hand gingerly over his swollen lips. "Brice hits awful damn' hard! When do I start work?"

"In the mornin'."

"I'll be there." Hoff turned and was half-way to the door when he halted and came back again. He glanced down at Frank with a veiled-over look in eyes, asking abruptly, "When's your next shipment of gold goin' down?"

Frank hesitated a brief moment before he replied, "Tomorrow."

"Take my tip and don't send along a shotgun. Brice has put spotters out, or rather Phenego has. Any rig loaded down with a guard will be stopped from now on. He has the men that can do it, too."

"Thanks for lettin' me know."

"It ain't costin' me nothin'," was Hoff's reply.

Once he was gone, Frank soberly considered the information the ex-Mountain driver had imparted. He had been wary of Hoff's question concerning the shipment of gold and given his answer accordingly. No gold was being shipped tomorrow. But, to test the reliability of the new crewman's word, tomorrow's stage would carry a weighted money chest and Hoff would be the driver. A guard would go along with Hoff, Ned Stiles probably. No, Frank decided, not Ned. He would go himself. Only by being with Hoff and judging him in the light of what happened on the trip could he make up his mind about him.

Still none too sure of Hoff, Frank could at least thank him for suggesting this way of proving him.

XI

THE NEXT morning's dawn was cold and clear and the peaks to the northward were mantled with the first fall of snow. A blue haze of wood smoke hung along the canyon and the air was crisp and fragrant with the odor of burning piñon and cedar. At seven the howl of the whistles at the mines in Jimtown faintly rode down the still air and this morning the puffing exhaust of the winch engines from the shaft houses up the slope threw back sharper echoes than those of yesterday. Winter was on the way.

Yates stopped by the yard early, a few minutes after Frank rolled out of his blankets. He was, he said, on the way up into the hills to buy hay. Frank watched the wrangler leave the yard, feeling strangely envious of the man, for this past week had broken the strict routine of a life that had hardened him to a fine-drawn toughness; he had to admit that he missed the grueling demands on his physical make-up that had been so much a part of his past five years and, could he have had the choice today, he would have liked to trade places with Yates and travel the hills alone and astride a tough horse.

That strong and alien regret was forgotten as he went down the street at six for his breakfast. Coming within sight of Mountain's ramp, he saw the big red-lettered banner stretched across the mouth of the high covered runway.

NEW LOW FARES
TICKET TO ALKALI ~~$18.00~~ $10.00
BAGGAGE FREE, MEAL FREE

Although he didn't pause as he passed the rival stageyard, he was studying that sign on which the old fare had been so boldly crossed out to be replaced with a new one cutting it nearly in half. This would be Brice's work, and it was obvious that Stagline would have to make a like reduction in fares. Over his meal Frank reasoned out the wisdom of Brice's move. It was designed primarily to cut into Stagline's passenger business. For a day or so it would.

But, beyond that, there was a basis of common sense to a low fare for the outtrip. Rarely did either Stagline's or Mountain's downgoing stages travel with a full load. Over half the people leaving Goldrock were too broke to afford the ride. They had come to the camp with high hopes and the reckless belief that to spend money was to make more. When that illusion finally vanished and they had to leave for a new country or starve, they carefully saved what scant resources they had left. The road down to the desert was dotted with stragglers afoot, headed out, and there was rarely a freight-hitch crossing the desert to Alkali that didn't bring along a few. This new low fare would mean that some of those weary disillusioned men would be riding the stages. So Brice had probably unknowingly struck upon an idea that would load every outgoing stage to the axles.

After breakfast Frank hunted up a sign painter and ordered a cross-street banner twice as large and ornate as Mountain's. He stopped in at Slater's harness shop directly across the street from Sam Osgood's office and, for a ten-dollar consideration, got Slater's consent to rope one end of the banner to the false front of his store. Then he went across the street and climbed the outside stairway to Osgood's office.

The lawyer was more than willing to let him anchor one end of the banner to the front wall of his office. Frank went on to tell him of the new contracts he'd brought back from Jimtown yesterday. Osgood was openly amazed at this stroke of luck. But he was at first wary of Frank and Belle using their title to the stage line as a bond for the two biggest mines.

"Supposin' something happens?" he asked. "You'd lose everything, and Belle . . . Well, you know how I feel about her."

"But she asked me to do it," Frank insisted. "At first I was in on it alone with the Combination. She combed me over because I hadn't used her half to get Belden's business."

Osgood's heavy brows lifted in a look of understanding. He smiled briefly. "She's changed a lot in two days," he said. Then, with a shrug, "It's up to her. If you can make it work, it'll put the outfit on its feet. Those Jimtown mines ship out one hell of a lot of bullion."

"There's sixty thousand going down on Friday."

The lawyer's face took on a grave look. "Make sure nothing happens."

With a nod Frank went on to the door. "Belle should be here in an hour or to sign the papers. Let me know when they're ready and I'll take 'em up to Belden and Shannon. We'll have to deposit the deed with the Alkali bank."

Back at the yard Frank inconspicuously set about getting ready for the drive with Hoff. Yesterday he had seen an old discarded money chest lying in a corner of Harmon's shop, nearly buried under a heap of scrap iron. He got six heavy canvas money sacks from the safe and filled them with iron filings swept from the floor around Harmon's workbench. The chest was loaded and locked and in the stage long before Hoff appeared.

At ten Hoff wheeled the mud wagon out into the street, with Frank on the seat beside him cradling a shotgun between his knees. Hoff put his teams with seeming recklessness through a narrow space between two loaded ore wagons and held them at a steady trot even through the heaviest traffic at the center of town. Before they had gone a hundred yards, Frank knew he was sitting beside a man who wasn't reckless but an expert.

They were beyond the hotel and drawing closer to the rumble of the stamps at the lower edge of town when a man hailed them from the walk, "Justice!"

Frank looked over there and saw George Chapin, the Wells-Fargo agent, waving to him. He spoke a word to Hoff, and the mud wagon slowed and rocked to a stop. Chapin came out from the end of a crowded tie rail, waited for a wagon to pass, and then over to the stage.

He took a banded fat wallet from his pocket and handed it up to Frank, along with an invoice pad, saying, "This goes down to the freight agent in Alkali. It's to cover a shipment coming in tomorrow."

Frank looked at the invoice, seeing that the wallet held three thousand dollars in bills. He put the wallet in his inside coat pocket, signed the invoice, and, with a "So long" from Chapin, they were once more traveling down the street.

Before they struck the climbing grade that led up to the mesa rim, Frank had Hoff stop the stage again. While Hoff eyed him quizzically, he climbed aground and opened the mud wagon's door and stepped up into it. He hesitated only a moment in deciding what he would do, finally acting on the hunch that had guided him in preparing for this trip that was to test Hoff. He reached down and rattled the padlock on the chest, pretending to be unlocking it. But he stuffed the wallet down behind a seat cushion and half a minute later was swinging up beside Hoff, drawling, "No sense in takin' chances."

The teams were slogging into the stiffest climb in the grade, half a mile farther on, before Hoff ventured any comment. "You're takin' a bigger chance ridin' a guard on a money chest," was his dry statement.

Frank made no answer to this reference to Hoff's advice of last night, choosing instead to let the man draw his own conclusions. After that neither of them spoke, Hoff holding the stubborn silence of hurt feelings, Frank merely waiting to see what was to happen.

It did happen. Twelve miles below town the road hung to a ledge above a boulder-strewn reach of the canyon bottom, making a sharp blind bend around a precipitous rise of the west wall. As they came into sight of the stretch of road beyond the bend, Hoff stiffened on the seat and lifted his boot to the brake, saying sharply, "Call the deal, boss! Here's trouble!"

Three riders blocked the trail ahead. One held a Winchester to his shoulder while sunlight glinted brightly from drawn six-guns in the hands of the other two. All three had their faces covered with bandannas and wore their hats tilted low.

Frank let go his hold on the shotgun, drawling, "Pull up." As he spoke, he lifted his hands.

Hoff, after one puzzled sideward glance at him, booted home the brake and tightened on the reins, cursing saltily at his horses. The lead team was within twenty feet of the nearest of the riders when the mud wagon came to a stop.

"Step down and stretch, gents!" drawled the leader of the trio. He motioned his two companions on to the coach and rode in close to the leaders and reached out to take a hold on the off-animal's bit ring.

Frank and Hoff climbed aground. The leader came around to Hoff's side as the other two swung down out of saddle. One of these came in behind Frank to lift the .38 from his holster, punch out the shells, and return it to his thigh again. Then he went through Frank's pockets, returning Frank's watch after an acid, "Not worth botherin' about." The other swung open the coach door, looked in, and called, "Here she sits, boss."

"Heave it out," the man with Hoff called from the opposite side, and presently the heavy money chest was thudding to the ground below the door.

A few muttered words sounded from Hoff's side of the coach. Then the outlaw over there was calling, "On your way, gents! And careful not to reach for that scatter-gun!"

Three minutes later as Frank looked back toward the bend, all that remained to mark the passage up the trail of the outlaws was a settling thin fog of dust.

Hoff said sourly, "You may know what you're doin'! I don't!"

Frank looked at the man, smiling thinly. "I was wrong, Hoff. I had to be sure you weren't runnin' a sandy. That chest was loaded with junk, stuff I swept up off the floor of Harmon's shanty this mornin'."

There was a visible break in the driver's flinty expression. Then worry gathered on his face. "But the Wells-Fargo wallet wasn't empty."

"No. I stuffed it down behind the cushion of the seat. You can drop me at the meadow below The Narrows and I'll get back to town. Get a receipt for the wallet when you deliver it."

A wry grin touched Hoff's face. He drawled, "You sure are a trustin' soul, Justice."

"What would you have done in my place? For all I knew, you and Brice framed that scrap last night so he could put a man on with me."

The driver's grin widened. "That wasn't no put-up job," he drawled. He laughed softly. "I'd sure like to see them three jaspers when they shoot the lock off that chest!"

"So would I." Frank felt the tension lessen between them and was thankful Hoff wasn't taking offense at what had happened. "From now on we don't send a guard with a money chest." After a moment he added one reservation, "Except for next Friday. Then we send every man and every gun I can lay hands on."

Frank was back in town two hours later,

riding a dun horse he'd borrowed from the corral in the meadow where Bob Aspen had pitched his tent. He was surprised to see Sam Osgood come out of the office and across the yard as he was off-saddling the dun, even more surprised when he caught the worry written on the lawyer's face.

"Something's happened to Belle," were Osgood's first words. "I waited until eleven for her to come to the office, then went up to her house. She isn't there. None of the neighbors have seen her this morning. There's something queer about it, Frank!"

"You could've missed her," Frank said. "She might have called at the office while you were away."

"She'd have left a note. The office was open." Osgood shook his head gravely. "Would you mind goin' up there to take a look? There were horse tracks in the yard. I think they may mean something."

A dull foreboding gathered in Frank at this last. He asked quickly, "There's a fence around the yard, isn't there? What would horses be doing in the yard?"

"There's probably some simple explanation. But I want you to go up there and see what you think."

Osgood was more worried than he let on. Frank pulled the cinch tight again and swung up into the saddle. "Where's Stiles?"

"At the doctor's with Fred Cash. I sent him, more to stop him from asking questions than anything else."

"When he gets back, send him along after me," Frank said, turning toward the gate.

He swung from the street into the narrow lane that climbed the canyon's gradual western slope. The Le Soeur house was the last in line, and as he rode up to the white-painted picket fence bordering the yard he was afraid of what he was to find.

There was sign, as Osgood had said. Late last night it had frozen to harden the ground softened by day before yesterday's rain. Yet he found clear deep imprints of three different sets of shoes close in before the wide porch of the small house. The answer was obvious; riders had been in the yard last night, before the freeze. The sign led around from the rear of the house, keeping wide of it as far as the back gate. Having followed it that far, Frank stood looking out beyond the picket fence, able to follow the line of hoof-churned earth up the slope for fifty yards before it was lost in the thin growth of sagebrush.

He went back to the house and onto the porch and cupped hands to his face, peering in through the front window. It took several seconds for his eyes to focus on the half-light of the room beyond. It was pleasantly, almost gaily, furnished, showing sign of a woman's colorful touch. Bright curtains hung at this window and the one at the east wall. Bright-colored Navajos livened the somberness of a varnished horsehair sofa.

Yet Frank wasn't more than vaguely aware of any of these things. What his glance settled on was an over-turned rocker on the floor in front of the stove. Sight of that quickened the slow beat of his pulse and sent a coolness through him. The rocker was striking evidence of violence in an otherwise neatly arranged room.

He went to the back of the house and there, peering in through the kitchen window, had more tangible evidence of what he already expected. The lamp in the kitchen was burning.

By the time Ned Stiles rode up the lane,

the sign in the yard had told Frank something more. One of the three ponies had been on a lead rope as he came into the yard. But this animal's track made a deeper imprint as it struck out up the slope with the other, lined toward the rim. Frank's eye, long practiced in reading sign, picked out this obscure detail and he knew the answer at once. The pony, led into the yard riderless, had carried someone away. And that rider, Frank was almost sure, had been Belle Le Soeur.

His first impulse was to tell Stiles everything, about the overturned rocker, the lighted lamp in the kitchen, and the lead horse. But as he crossed the yard to the front gate, he thought of Osgood and knew that there was little point in worrying Belle's friend until he had something more definite to go on.

So he told the redhead, "There's nothin' here to worry anybody. Tell Osgood I'll stop at his office later in the day."

"What about that sign he mentioned?"

Frank lifted his shoulders in an offhand gesture as he lied blandly. "The back gate was open. Looks to me like a horse must have busted a hobble string and strayed

154

up here to have a feed on the grass in the yard."

Stiles looked yardward. "Pretty slim pickin's," he drawled.

"But slimmer outside the fence." Frank stepped up into the saddle, adding, "Look after things at the layout, Ned. I've got some steam to work off and I'm goin' to see what's back up yonder." He lifted a hand toward the rim and the farther hills.

Ned Stiles smiled meagerly, said "Sure," and turned back down the lane. He had detected restlessness and a worry behind Frank's casual manner. He wondered about Belle Le Soeur, trying to think where she could have gone. He was almost down to the street before he remembered leaving Belle at the doorway to Mountain's waiting room last night. Then, because there seemed no connection between Belle's call on Ed Brice last night and the matter at hand, he forgot about it.

From the rim Frank watched Ned turn out of sight into the street. He lifted his reins and rode several rods along the rounded crest of the rim. Presently he came on the sign that was now as familiar to him as that of the horses on his lost ranch back home. He lifted the dun into a trot, following the line of that sign as it struck straight back toward the higher hills. His face was set bleakly and he found the old habit returning of scanning closely the ground ahead. Topping the first high knoll half a mile back from the rim, he put the dun into an abrupt lope, not wanting to sky-line himself longer than necessary.

It was beyond the knoll that he reined in long enough to reload his .38. He had almost forgotten that it had been emptied this morning.

XII

HAVING LEFT Frank at the meadow after putting new teams into the harness, Hoff had been in no particular hurry once a turning in the trail hid him from Bob Aspen's tent beyond the corral. He hadn't had the appearance of a driver interested in impressing his new boss with record time for the Alkali run, as Fred Cash had on the uptrip last night. In fact, Hoff had no intention of taking Stagline's mud wagon to Alkali today.

A mile and a half below the meadow

station, he braked the coach and swung sharply from the road and down off its shoulder into the mouth of a faintly marked and brush-choked trail leading over toward the canyon's steep-climbing west wall. A tangle of tough scrub oak and wild hackberry seemed to block the trail so as to make it impassable for the mud wagon, but Hoff put his teams through it until he came to an open patch of ground. Looking back, he saw that the brush hid the road. He booted the brake, wound his reins around the socketed whip, and dropped leisurely aground.

The first thing he did was to climb in the door and search behind the seat cushions until he found the Wells-Fargo wallet. Then, more leisurely, he went up to the off-leader to buckle a harness strap that had worked loose; he unwound a turned rein and straightened it back through the ring on the swing animal's collar. Finally he took out tobacco and stepped over to squat in the shade of a cedar as he built a smoke.

Twenty minutes later, finishing his second cigarette, the sound of a horse coming down off the slope toward him lifted his glance upward. Presently a rider on a bay horse moved through the brush close by and came into the clearing. He was the outlaw who had been with Hoff on the side of the stage opposite Frank an hour ago during the holdup. What Hoff had whispered to him then had brought him down here.

He saw Hoff sitting there and gave a meager grin, saying as he came up, "You weren't runnin' a sandy?"

For his answer Hoff reached to the pocket of his coat and took out the wallet. The rider's eyes widened as he saw it. Then his smile broadened and he drawled, "We saw Chapin give it to you in town and done some plain and fancy cussin' when it wasn't in the chest. What happened to it?"

"Justice had stuffed it down behind a seat inside. I had the hunch he was givin' in too easy. Otherwise I wouldn't have told you to meet me here."

"It took some figurin' to get what you meant. What made you so spooky?"

"Justice. He wasn't any too sure of me. But he is now."

"Went back, did he?"

Hoff nodded and held out the wallet. "There's three thousand here. See that it gets to Phenego . . . all of it."

Quick belligerence came to the rider's face. But if his first impulse had been to resent Hoff's implication, his second, the wiser, was to ignore it. Something in Hoff's manner carried an unmistakable warning. The rider nodded, thrust the wallet into his shirt, and turned back into the brush.

A quarter hour later he had topped the rim and was a mile beyond it, rounding a high broad outcropping, when his bay suddenly shied. The next moment he drew rein and slowly lifted his hands. Twenty feet away, his gray gelding hugging the shadow of the outcropping, squatted a man with a carbine held raised to his massive shoulder. As he came slowly erect he was a towering shape, as big a man as Phenego's rider had ever seen.

He drawled, "What's the hurry?" and let the stock of the rifle fall to the toe of his boot. When Phenego's man made no reply, he added, "Just toss it across."

"Toss what?"

"The money."

The other's face flushed. "Like hell!" he began. But, when the carbine muzzle nosed up at him again and caught the surface dullness to the pair of pale blue eyes

159

watching him, he reached into his shirt for the wallet and dropped it into the dust.

The big man said, "On your way. Your side-kicks are waitin' a mile above."

But the other didn't move. Some of the color was gone from his face and after a long moment he said, acidly, "Mind tellin' me how you were onto it?"

The big man said, "Two can play the game. Phenego ain't the only one with his eyes open."

"Who else?"

"Now that'd be givin' it away, wouldn't it?" the big man drawled tonelessly. "So long."

Still Phenego's rider made no move to pick up his reins. "I can't go back," he said abruptly, low-voiced. "They wouldn't believe me." His look held a trace of naked fear at the turn his mind was taking.

"Phenego can be an unforgivin' son." The big man waited a moment for his statement to carry its full weight. Then, "There's that local due in Alkali at four. If you killed a couple horses, you could make it."

"That's an idea." There was no trace of anger in the other's voice now as he weighed the suggestion. He seemed to have forgotten that this big man was the cause of his having to throw over a good job and leave the country.

Abruptly he touched spurs to the bay's flanks and wheeled the animal around, heading into the south instead of north, the direction he'd been taking.

The man on the gray watched him go and sat listening until the bay's gradually muted hoof-drum faded into the stillness. Then he stepped ponderously into the saddle and turned down into the canyon and headed for Goldrock.

Hoff, driving the mud wagon back toward the meadow corral, caught the faint echo of the gray's going ahead along the trail. The sound made Hoff faintly uneasy for several moments, until he told himself he'd imagined the sound. He looked down at the splintered edge of a round hole through the footboard. Back there in the brush he had drawn the .45 from the spring holster at his left armpit and shot once, placing the bullet nicely, he decided. The hole through the footboard would be the most convincing proof he could offer to bear out his story of how he'd lost the money.

He was using his whip and his three

teams were at a slogging run when he rolled in off the trail toward Bob Aspen's tent in the meadow a short time later. He saw no sign of life around the tent and bawled lustily, "Aspen! Get down here!"

A faint halloo answered him from the near slope. But he had to wait a full half minute before Bob Aspen appeared running down through the thin stand of timber edging the meadow. Aspen was out of breath when he came in past the corral.

Hoff let him get that far before he bawled, "Damn it, why ain't you on the job! They stopped me three miles below. Put a shot so close to my foot I damn' near lost a toe!" He pointed down to the hole in the footboard. "How in hell they knew, I can't figure. But they made me fork over that Wells-Fargo money!"

Bob Aspen's face went pale. Earlier, as he had helped Hoff harness, Hoff had talked enough to let the boy know how things were going with Stagline. Aspen had looked off toward the corral, where Frank Justice was throwing a saddle on a horse. In the hour or so Hoff had been gone, he had thought much of Frank and, in the worshipful way of youth, Frank Justice

162

had assumed heroic proportions in his mind. Hadn't the new boss knocked out Cliff Havens in that brawl at the Paradise the other night? And wasn't Havens known all through this country as being handier with his fists than any man who had ever struck this camp?

Now, with the stunning news Hoff was giving him, young Aspen's anger boiled over. "Why didn't you go for your iron?" he cried.

"With them same three jaspers looking at me across their sights?" Hoff laughed mirthlessly. "Hell, no! Do I look like that kind of a lughead?" He lifted the reins and kicked off the brake. "I'm headed for town!"

By the time the dust of the fast-climbing stage had settled in a still sun-bright air, the weakness that had first hit Bob Aspen's knees had gone and his riot of thought had become a more sober reasoning. All that remained was a cold fury toward Hoff, whom he'd never liked. He saw in the loss of the Wells-Fargo wallet a clear betrayal of the man who had two nights ago helped Burkitt at the time of the accident and almost single-handedly whipped Mountain's crew; he saw it as disloyalty toward the man who had licked Cliff Havens and this morning outguessed Phenego's hired killers. What was to happen to Stagline, to Frank Justice, now? To Bob Aspen this was the beginning of the outfit's slow ruin.

He saw in Hoff the embodiment of all Stagline's hard luck. He disliked the man's sour disposition and his biting tongue. He couldn't help but think that if Frank had been driving, even if Ned Stiles or he himself had been at the ribbons, things wouldn't have turned out this way.

He had arrived at this dead end in his reasoning when he remembered that faint echo of a shot that had come up to him while he was climbing the hill behind the meadow nearly half an hour ago. It puzzled him. He supposed at first that he had heard the shot that put the bullet hole through the mud wagon's footboard. But hadn't Hoff said the robbery had taken place three or four miles below? A man couldn't hear the sound of a six-gun at that distance along the canyon's twisting corridor.

A small doubt hardened in Aspen's mind. Had Hoff been telling the truth? Because he distrusted the man, he ran over to the corral and put a bridle and a hackamore on a pony and started down the road. Within a mile after leaving the camp, he pulled the horse down out of its hard run and began looking at the sign on the trail.

Minutes later he saw the marks of the stage's iron tires swing down off the road and enter the beginnings of a brush-choked side trail. Following that branching, he came to a place where the brush ringed a small clearing scarred with the marks of hoofs and boot soles. He slid from the horse's back and studied the sign more closely. Finally he found the shoeprints of a single horse leading down out of the brush at the back of the clearing. Over by the brush were two cigarette stubs, their papers different. Lastly sunlight glittered from a bright object and he came down off his horse to pick an empty shell case from the sand. And suddenly he understood that Hoff himself had shot the hole in the mud wagon's footboard.

Back at the meadow, after holding his horse at a full-out run the whole distance, he threw a spare saddle on another pony and headed up the road for town.

Ned Stiles was living up to the promise of his brick-red hair. "Why in the name o' God would they stop you again?" he blazed.

Hoff said meekly, "The way I figure it, they must've spotted Chapin givin' us that money this mornin'. When they stopped us the first time, they naturally thought the money was in the chest. They didn't break it open till we'd gone on, so they rode the rim and caught up with me again and made another try. I'm sure sorry, Stiles."

"Sorry!" Ned paced the broad doorway of the blacksmith shop. "What good does that do us when we lose our Wells-Fargo business? Why does Frank have to be gone at a time like this!"

Hoff left him alone and went on across to the stables, where Harmon needed help backing the mud wagon in under its shed. Ned watched him go, his look black with impotent rage. He felt he was somehow to blame for having let Hoff take the stage down this morning. He couldn't help but think that his being there might have made a difference. He could have put up a fight.

166

He knew he would be wasting time to set out on Frank's trail. So he went down the street to Sam Osgood's office. The lawyer's reception of the news matched his own. They decided not to notify Chapin until they'd talked with Frank.

Back on the street again, Ned turned into the first saloon he passed, the Queen. He took two quick drinks at the bar and lingered over a third. Liquor usually eased his mind, but now it seemed to have little effect on him. He had a fourth and a fifth glass as late afternoon's shadows thickened on the street. Then he bought a bottle and took it to the far end of the bar, where he could be comparatively alone.

Later, a barkeep, lighting the lamps at the end of the bar's mirror, said to him, "Better go easy, friend."

Stiles pushed the half-empty bottle away from him. "What's wrong with this rot-gut?" he growled. "No kick to it!" He felt as sober as before his first drink.

He wasn't hungry but decided he'd better eat. He was stepping out from the bar when Bob Aspen hurried up to him.

"Hiyuh, kid," Ned said. "Have a drink."

Without answering that the boy poured out his story, what he had learned on his

ride down from the meadow this afternoon. At first Stiles listened with keen attention. Then, as his fury mounted, he
felt the liquor hit him in a shocking wave.
He had to reach out to steady himself
against the bar. He listened without interrupting until Aspen had finished.

"So he double-crossed us!" Ned's voice
was slurred now. He reached out, pushed
Aspen aside with a sweep of his arm, and
headed for the door.

"Wait!" Aspen laid a hold on his arm.

But Ned jerked free and, shouldering
aside two men who blocked his way, made
for the street.

Bob Aspen followed, wisely keeping his
distance. He knew enough about this redheaded 'puncher not to try to stop him
now. He hung on Ned's heels all the way
back up the street to Stagline's gate. There
Ned suddenly wheeled on him and said
softly, "Kid, keep clear of me from now
on out!" The way he spoke left no doubt
that he meant what he said.

So Bob Aspen didn't go beyond the gate
but watched Ned walk back and disappear
in the darkness near the bunkhouse. Then
the bunkhouse door opened to momentarily outline Ned's short frame. As it

closed, something went out of Bob Aspen. The muscles along his overgrown boy's frame tightened. He listened for the sound of a shot.

Hoff wasn't in the bunkhouse. No one was. The lamp was burning in token of a recent occupant, probably Harmon. Thought of Harmon sent Ned to the blacksmith's bunk. Under the head of the mattress he found what he was looking for. It was a .44 Smith and Wesson with the barrel shortened to a three-inch length. Ned tilted open the frame, saw the brassy rims of five shells, and closed the gun again. He thrust it through the waistband of his pants beneath his coat and went out into the darkness. After the oppressive warmth of the bunkhouse, the night's settling chill had a sobering effect on him.

Going out the gate, he made out Bob Aspen's shadowy outline at the fence corner. He drawled, "I mean it, kid! Stay clear of me!" and went on down the path toward the store awnings.

The lanterns were swinging to a faint breeze in front of the Paradise. As Ned turned in there, Ed Walters passed on the street driving Stagline's inbound stage toward the yard. The walk here was crowded as the traffic slowed, listening to the calls of a barker who stood on a high stand extolling the merits of the entertainment offered beyond the doors. The way Stiles plodded straight into the crowd made men step quickly out of his way. Those he had to shoulder aside moved clear of him as they caught the set expression on his face. He elbowed the saloon's swing doors wide and stepped in through them as the barker gave him a wary glance and nodded down at a near-by houseman, who sauntered in close to Ned's heels.

Stiles felt the presence of the man behind him and, clear of the doors, wheeled about suddenly, breathing, "On your way!"

"Says who?" The houseman bridled. Then, catching the clouded-over expression in Ned's pale blue eyes, he edged off into the crowd by the bar.

Ned's mouth was dry. He bought a drink and felt the warm impact of liquor settle through him in a warning wave. Everything he did, even the movement of the crowd about him, seemed drawn to an unnatural slowness. He told himself that he was sober, that his excitement was what heightened every detail. He felt fine. He pressed his right elbow in at his waist feeling the hard outline of the gun underneath his coat. He stepped deliberately out from the bar and started down the teeming broad aisle between it and the gambling layouts.

The place was beginning to fill up. Yet there was plenty of room for a man to move around without being crowded. His glance went to the wall and to a window behind an empty blackjack layout farther down. He hoped he'd finish his errand here before a dealer opened play there.

If he'd been asked why he was so sure he was to find Hoff here, he couldn't have given an answer. Yet when he saw Hoff's thin shape, back turned to him, leaning against the free-lunch counter back by the empty dance floor, he wasn't even faintly surprised. He cuffed his Stetson onto the back of his head as he sauntered over there.

Three paces from the man he called softly, "Hoff!"

XIII

Hoff had stayed at the yard for an hour after Ned had left. Quiet by habit, the restlessness of his mind had made him unnaturally talkative as he followed Harmon back to the blacksmith shop after helping push the stage in under its shed. He sat on Harmon's anvil.

"Sooner or later I'll bump into them three," he drawled as Harmon went over to work the bellows of the forge. "And when I do . . ."

He paused intentionally, hoping Harmon would finish for him. But the blacksmith's broad back moved up and down to the stroke of the bellows handle and he said nothing.

"Blow a hole through my foot, would they!" Hoff went on. "By God, my time'll come! I ain't never thought I'd take pleasure in shootin' a man down. But I've changed my mind. I'd draw on them polecats on sight, take 'em on one at a time or all three at once!"

Still Harmon said nothing. He reached over to the workbench for a pair of tongs and thrust a cold iron shoe into the red coals in the forge.

"Justice ain't goin' to like this, is he, Harmon?" Hoff decided on a question that demanded an answer.

"Don't reckon he is."

Something in Harmon's tone made Hoff say querulously, "You talk like it was my fault! Who's goin' to make a play while starin' down the bore of a hog-leg?"

Harmon turned slowly to face the driver. He said mildly, "No one said you done wrong. And there's no call to tell me how tough you are. We've got a couple of gents workin' right here that have all the hair on their chests they need! But they don't crow over it. You're steamed up over nothin'. Go on down the street and have a drink and cool off."

Hoff looked sullen for a moment, but since Harmon's back was turned again he finally found no point in it. He wanted to say something else. But there was nothing he could think of, so he went out across the yard and onto the street. He wanted to see Phenego but remembered the saloonman's warning not to come openly to the Paradise. He found he was hungry, so he turned in at a restaurant and ordered a big meal. Finished with it, he loafed along the street until it got dark, then walked in between two buildings and back to the alley that ran behind the Paradise. Presently he was knocking on the alley door of Phenego's office.

It was Phenego who let him in. He was alone in the office. Phenego's first question was abrupt. "Where's Richter?"

Hoff's frown showed his puzzlement. He shrugged. "Didn't he show up?"

Phenego made no reply but went to his desk to take a cigar from the box there. He bit the end from the cigar and forgot to light it. Suddenly he burst out, "What's goin' on here? Two hours ago it was the Le Soeur girl missin'! Now this!"

"Belle Le Soeur missin'?" Hoff queried. "Since when?"

Phenego gave an irritable wave of the hand. "What do you care? Since last night. Faunce is up there now, goin' through the house with Sam Osgood. I'd give—" He broke off, wheeling sharply on Hoff. "Did you turn that money over to Richter?" Without waiting, he answered his own question. "You wouldn't be loco enough to show up here if you hadn't!"

Hoff drawled, "You ain't said yet what

happened. Where's the pair that were sidin' Richter?"

"Where they belong, out of sight! Richter told 'em to wait for him and went on alone to meet you. That's the last they saw of him. They found his sign, nothin' else. Someone stopped him after he left you, someone with boots the size of a wagon bed! But from then on Richter's sign headed south out of the hills. Reno and Ed followed him five miles before they lost his sign on the main road."

"He must've headed out with the money."

"He wouldn't do that without a reason, would he?" Phenego said savagely. "There's only one answer. He was made to turn over the money and got buck fever on comin' back with a lame story." He motioned curtly with a tilt of his grizzled head to the office's inner door. "Go on; leave me alone. I want to think this out."

Hoff's bewilderment was so engrossing that he forgot Phenego's warning of not being seen around the office. He went to the lunch counter at the near end of the bar and asked for a cup of coffee.

He was reaching for the cup when Ned Stiles, behind him, called softly, "Hoff!"

He wheeled instantly around, his elbow overturning his cup. He thought he had detected a warning note in Stiles' voice, but nevertheless his face relaxed from its tight set and he began, "You scared the . . ." Then he saw the look in Ned's eyes and stabbed his right hand in under his coat.

Ned caught the beginning of that move and his own hand brushed his coat aside and he reached for Harmon's gun. He'd never practiced the draw much and what little he had was with a thigh holster. But in this moment, as the threat he faced cleared the alcohol fog from his brain, his every move was sure and swift.

The .44's balance felt smooth, its butt plates snug to his palm. The hammer tension seemed feather-light so that he didn't know the exact instant it slipped from under the ball of his thumb. The kick of the weapon came as a surprise, for he had been staring for long seconds, it seemed, into the round bore of Hoff's Colt. He saw the Colt buck upward as it lanced smoke and flame. He felt a tug at his left sleeve. Behind him a man screamed.

All at once Hoff's eyes were wide-staring, full of instant terror. His long-fingered hands clawed open and clutched at his chest. He was falling, brokenly, in a slow-wheeling totter. Only when he had slid down onto the floor at full length did Ned Stiles spin about, heading for the window behind the blackjack table at a run.

He stumbled over a man lying on the floor, the man Hoff's bullet had struck down. He fell to his knees but was up again the next instant. Behind him a gun exploded deafeningly. On the wall ahead a long splinter of wood was flicked loose and dropped floorward as he reached for the stool at the blackjack layout and flung it through the window. He faced the room briefly as he vaulted backward through the window. He cut his hand on a jagged splinter of glass, dropping quickly groundward, trying to beat the down-drop of a gun in the hand of the apron behind the end of the bar.

The bullet that was intended for him struck the sill of the window a split second after his head had dropped below it. The slug ricocheted up the side passageway in a high whine as he headed alleyward, thrusting the gun back into his belt. He found his steps none too steady now. He turned the back corner of the saloon and was in the alley. He found it hard to breathe but kept on running until his lungs fought for air. He caught faintly the sound of shouting behind him along the alley as he slowed to a walk. Now his left arm stung fiercely; his shirt sleeve under his coat felt cool and wet and he knew Hoff's bullet had grazed him.

He was beyond the stores, and the alley had become a narrow wagon lane butting the depth of the shallow lots behind the makeshift houses. He heard the shouts of the Paradise men behind strengthening now and broke into a tired trot. Then he saw the kitchen light of Helen Moreford's house and ran in toward it. Halfway across the small yard he stopped abruptly, knowing he couldn't go in there.

He faced the alley and the sound of men coming along it. His hand lifted toward the gun at his belt. Then his glance took in the small shed behind the Moreford house. And, as the first swinging lantern came in sight down the alley, outlining the shapes of Phenego's men, he ran across to the shed, turned the pegged stop on the door, and stepped inside. He struck a match and looked about him. Neatly filling the shed's rear half was a head-high stack of cordwood that filled all the space between the planks of a half-loft and the floor. At one side of the door sat a battered trunk, and a broken hoe leaned against the wall in that corner.

The match's feeble flare showed him a short length of twisted baling wire hanging from a nail on a wall stud. He bent the wire straight, pulled the door tight shut, and pushed the wire through the crack to work the door peg down until it held the panel firmly. Then he groped his way across the shed in the dark, hearing angry voices close outside. Reaching up, he caught a hold on the loft planking and swung up and belly-down onto it. By the time a fist pounded loudly on the back door of the Moreford house close by, he was lying across the planks, stretched at full length, his gun lined down through the darkness toward the slitted line of feeble lantern light that outlined the doorway.

He heard Helen Moreford's voice. She was arguing with someone out there, but he wasn't able to catch even a fragment of what was said. A voice he at once knew was Cliff Havens' spoke up. Then the house door slammed and the men moved off across the yard and he thought they were gone. But at that moment someone fumbled at the peg on the shed door and the door swung open. Ned drew his head and shoulders back of the plank's edge barely in time to keep from being seen in the orange outwash of a lantern's light.

"Let's catch up with the others, Reno," said a gruff voice. "This is a waste o' time. The thing was locked on the outside."

The door banged shut. Whoever closed it didn't bother to turn the peg, for it slowly swung open a foot and stayed that way. Looking out through it, Ned started breathing again as the lantern's light faded and the blackness out there became absolute.

The afternoon had brought a slow-gathering sense of bitter defeat to Frank. By the time he stood his horse below the westward rounded lip of the valley and looked down on Jimtown and across at the mines under the cliff rim opposite, he knew that he was licked. Belle Le Soeur had disappeared as completely as though the sign he'd lost at midafternoon had never been there.

He judged he had ridden better than twenty miles since leaving the Le Soeur yard in Goldrock. For the first hour there had seemed some purpose in the way the sign was leading. But at the end of that hour, when the tracks of the three horses wound aimlessly down the sandy beds of a tangle of dry washes footing a high *barranco,* he began to have his doubts. Later, when the sign faded across a lower rock-gaunt wasteland and he lost it for good, he knew that the riders who held Belle prisoner had made this long detour for the sole purpose of confusing anyone on their back trail.

The next two hours he had spent trying to ride the limits of that stretch of country where wind and water had cleaned most of the topsoil from the bedrock. In the end he'd had to give it up. He had struck deeper and upward into the hills, reluctant to carry such discouraging news back to Sam Osgood but having no choice.

He was convinced of one thing, that whoever had broken into Belle's house last night had had a sole purpose—that of making it impossible for Stagline to turn over a signed deed as a bond for the Jimtown mines. Without Belle's signature on the deed, Frank doubted that even he could go ahead with the necessary arrangements with Shannon, let alone those with Belden which called for Belle's consent. So there was but one obvious answer; the party injured most by Frank's contracts with the mines was the one responsible for Belle's disappearance—and that man was Matt Phenego.

As he rode the hills with the lowering sun's light at his back, he saw that there was but one solution to the troubles gradually strangling Stagline. He must see Phenego again. This time he would go without any offer but that of a finish fight. He supposed it would be impossible for him to face Phenego alone, but he would try. If he succeeded, the outcome would be decided by a gun. It didn't enter his mind to try and guess who would come out of such a meeting alive. All he wanted was his chance.

Now he rode down the slope and into the valley in the fading light, cutting obliquely southward toward the Goldrock road. He caught a flash of light from one of the shaft houses across the basin and at first thought it was a lantern. But as it dimmed he knew he was seeing the reflection of the setting sun.

The old habit of riding head down,

studying the ground close ahead, had become strong in him this afternoon. He was doing it, idly, without thinking, as he rode the downward flank of a jack-pine belt toward the center of the valley.

He almost went on without recognizing the dark lined splotch of sign on the ground and he cut across it. His pony had taken two full strides before he reined in sharply and turned back to have another look. Then his first tension eased off and he laughed softly, knowing that for days now he would have that feeling each time he saw a hoofprint clear on the ground. The intensity of his earlier search was carrying over now that that search was ended.

Still, he bent low in the saddle to study the hoofprints in the half-light. What he saw made him jump aground and kneel alongside the sign.

The hackles rose along the channel of his spine as he read the unmistakable pattern he'd followed earlier in the afternoon. There was the print of the broken shoe. Almost beside it was the toed-out mark left by the horse he had decided was the one Belle rode.

He straightened, his glance running out along the line the horses had taken last night. Then, after the tracks faded into the obscurity of the dimming light, he looked up and ahead and was seeing the cluster of shabby buildings that was Jimtown a mile distant.

He squatted there and rolled a smoke, the dun's reins looped over his arm. He cupped the match as he lit the quirly and eyed the vague shadows of the false-fronted buildings bleakly, wondering what secrets they held for him.

When it was totally dark, when the lights shone down from the barracklike bunkhouses of the mines across the valley, he stood stiffly erect to ease his cramped muscles. Presently he climbed stiffly into the saddle. He put the dun out across the sage-studded valley floor toward the town.

From high beyond the cliffs to the east sounded the mournful night chant of a hunting coyote. A late-working steam winch in one of the shaft houses chugged mutedly, the sound heightening the stillness.

That same stillness held on as he rode the beginnings of Jimtown's narrow street. The fronts of the deserted buildings threw back echoes of his pony's slow stomp. The town seemed utterly dead, deserted. He started at sight of a scurrying small shadow blacker than the darkness in under a sagging store awning. Then he smiled thinly, recognizing it as a hunting cat.

He was almost abreast the faded awning sign of the saloon before he caught a faint sliver of light along the sill of the boarded-up door. He paused there in the middle of the street, having the abrupt feeling that he was being watched, that he wasn't as alone as he'd thought. Then he reined over toward the broken hitching rail in front of the saloon. He was deliberate as he came aground, even more deliberate in the way he tied the dun's reins to the sagging pole.

His boots sent hollow echoes down the street's brief corridor as he crossed the rotting plank walk to the boarded-up door. The jingle of his spurs seemed loud, so oppressive was the stillness. Now he could see light more plainly through the shrunken board sheathing.

He pulled at the edge of those boards and wasn't surprised when they swung easily outward. There was no squeak of rusty hinges and in this small sign of the door's recent usage he had his proof that life hadn't entirely left Jimtown. Inside were slatted swing doors, with a knee-high wedge of faint lamplight showing from under them.

He pushed the batwings aside and was in a narrow low room. It was uncertainly lighted by a single lamp over the center of a bar running halfway the length of the right wall. In the cavernous vague background were tables with legs-up chairs piled on them. A big mail-order calendar hung awry against a cracked and high mirror across from the bar. Everything in the room was coated with dust and around the cuspidors scattered at random along the walls and bar were litters of tobacco shreds, wheat-straw cigarette papers, and filth.

Three men stood in front of the bar, another behind it. A whisky bottle sat on the grimy counter to one side of a face-up array of soiled cards. One of the trio of customers was a giant in stature. The man behind the bar was the only one who glanced at Frank as he came in, and that glance was brief.

As Frank sauntered over to the near end of the bar, the big man slapped a card down and drawled, "Pay me, boys." His voice boomed hollowly and with a strong resonance.

There was a general breaking up of the

game. Frank caught the barkeep's eye and said, "Make mine bourbon."

The man gave a brief negative move of his bald head. "No bourbon." His tone was final.

"Rye, then," Frank told him.

"No rye."

Frank glanced at the bottle, at others on a shelf behind the bar. "Corn?"

"No corn."

Frank tilted his head toward the bottle on the bar. "What's that?"

"Private bottle," came the easy answer. "This place closed down two years ago, stranger."

Frank felt the big man's eyes on him, eyes that were a pale blue and inscrutable. He waited a moment for the offer of a drink; when it didn't come, he said, "Then you can give me something else. Where'll I find Belle Le Soeur?"

He was watching the big man, whose eyes showed nothing but faint wonderment. Then the man was drawling, "Now that's a pretty name. Should it mean somethin' to us?"

His companion behind him said smoothly, softly, "What the hell, Roy; it's four to one! Let's have some fun!"

XIV

FOR LONG minutes after the light outside the shed door had faded, Stiles lay listening for any sound that might betray the presence of a man left behind by Phenego's crew. Satisfied finally that there was no one in the yard, he shifted around until he was sitting, head hunched under the rafters. He took off his coat and rolled up his left sleeve and felt a cooler wetness along his arm. It smarted painfully, but when he moved the arm the soreness seemed to be in the skin, not deep in the muscle, and he concluded that the bullet had only burned him.

He wrapped his bandanna around the arm and took it between his teeth to pull the knot tight. He was sitting that way, doubled over, his bad arm thrust back over his opposite shoulder, when feeble light showed through the door's open wedge.

He quickly drew his feet up and went belly-down on the planking again. Abruptly Helen Moreford's voice shuttled plainly across from the house. Her words were tense under an emotion he couldn't understand.

"I don't believe it, Ed!"

Even before Ed Brice's voice spoke, Ned knew who the man was with her. Brice asked querulously, "Where are you going?"

"For some wood."

Brice said, "I'll go with you."

"I can manage, thanks." By Helen's tone Ned could tell that she was on edge, for he knew her well.

Regardless of her reply, Brice's heavier boot tread blended with hers and approached the shed.

Suddenly the door was creaking open. Ned lifted his head a fraction of an inch and had a brief glimpse of Helen stepping in through the doorway, the shadow of Brice's taller bulk beyond the opening. The girl's slight shape was rigidly erect, giving her a look of slenderness. The expression on her oval face was tense and pale; he thought he could read fear in her eyes but wasn't sure. Then he dropped his head out of the lantern's reach of light in fear that Brice would see him.

A moment later Helen was breathing intently, "You know something, Ed. You keep holding it over me, like . . . like a club!"

"Isn't that puttin' it pretty strong?" Brice drawled smoothly, and his tone was humble. "I thought we were gettin' on fine, Helen."

"You've been kind." Helen sounded contrite now. "But it's there, nevertheless. You know how I feel, Ed. You must know how I feel about this."

"Meanin' there's someone else?" There was a moment's pause before Brice added, "Stiles? He killed a man tonight."

"If he did, the man deserved it. What if I do like him?" Helen was immediately on the defensive. "But that doesn't answer this other. What do you know about Roy?"

"Should I know somethin'?" There was no longer that humbleness in Brice's voice. It had been replaced by an edge of irritation.

"You keep hinting that something's going on I don't know about. What is it? Tell me."

"There isn't anything to tell."

"Is he . . . is he mixed up with those men that hang out around Jimtown?"

"Is he?" It was hard to detect admission in Brice's bland question, but it was there.

"I knew it," the girl breathed, sensing the indictment Brice had placed against her brother more fully than Ned could. "We left home because he got into trouble. He's . . . he's weak, Ed."

"Weak nothin'! He's about the biggest man I ever laid eyes on," Brice said quietly.

"I don't mean that!" Helen flared. "I mean he'll do things like . . . like taking this job as watchman and using it to cover something else." There was outright bitterness in the girl's words. "Is he one of Phenego's men?" she asked abruptly.

Brice's reply was a long time coming. "I don't know, Helen."

A thud on the planking beneath him tightened every muscle in Ned's slight frame. But then he heard a scraping sound and knew that Helen was taking down firewood from the stack beneath the half-loft.

Presently Brice said, "Here, let me do it," and for several moments no word was spoken and Ned had sound alone to tell him that Brice was gathering an arm-load of the split cedar.

They were gone before Ned was quite

aware of it. The light faded and the door closed gently and he heard the peg being turned. Then, as he was pushing up to lift his legs over the loft edge, Helen said, "Leave it on the porch, Ed. Good night."

"You're not sore, Helen?" Brice asked. "If I knew anything, I'd tell it."

"That's not the truth, Ed," came Helen's quiet accusing tones, followed by the gentle closing of the house door.

As Brice's steps faded across the yard, there was a high elation in Ned. He hadn't known until now how much this girl had been in his thoughts. He hadn't seen her in four days. A sense of frustration and his belief that Helen was more than mildly interested in Brice had, he understood now, changed him. It had been partly responsible for the unreasoning rage in him that had resulted in his shooting Hoff tonight. He didn't regret having tried to kill a man, particularly Hoff; but he could see where Helen Moreford had assumed more than a casual importance in his thoughts.

She cared for him! That one fact rose over all the others he had learned in these last few moments. With this sobering realization a subtle change came over Ned Stiles and his mind was no longer dulled under the brooding and worry of the past few days. He felt almost lighthearted. But that emotion was short-lived as he remembered what Brice had the same as admitted concerning Roy Moreford.

Until now Ned had liked and admired Roy. A giant of a man with a hearty booming laugh, Helen's brother and he had a lot in common. They were both irresponsible and a little wild, both were cow-country men. Ned hadn't found it strange that Roy took the first easy job he could find—that of watchman at the Oriole, a shut-down mine up in Jimtown. He himself had never cared to work his guts out grubbing for gold the way most of the men in this boom camp did and he understood why Roy would scorn that way of earning a living. If he had thought it queer that Roy left Helen alone most of the time, it hadn't occurred to him until now.

The implications behind Brice's words were sinister. It was known that the riff-raff and outlaws of this country hung out in Jimtown since it had become nothing but a huddle of abandoned buildings. Rumor had it that a man could still buy a drink in Jimtown's boarded-up saloon, and Ned had no doubts but that

Roy knew the place. It wouldn't be strange, either, if Roy had a speaking acquaintance with the men who frequented the place. But it stretched Ned's imagination to suppose that Roy traveled with the outlaws. Still there must be some basis of fact behind Brice's accusation.

He saw now how Brice had blackmailed the girl with whatever he knew about her brother and his respect for Brice suffered a severe letdown. The impulse to discover the truth about Roy Moreford was all at once strong in him. So strong that he had swung down off the loft before he quite knew what he intended to do about it.

He thought at first of going to the house to talk with Helen. But he decided that she knew little about her brother beyond the vague something Brice had implied. Then he thought of riding up to Jimtown and, ignoring the threat of the Paradise men who might still be hunting him, he groped along the wall until he found the twisted piece of baling wire and thrust it through the crack in the door and pushed up the peg.

Minutes later the lantern on Stagline's office shed showed him a man carrying a shotgun pacing the platform. He smiled thinly, guessing correctly that Jim Faunce had probably deputized a few men and put one here at the yard on the chance that he would come after a horse to make a getaway.

He went on openly past the gate, not even bothering to cross the street where the thicker shadow offered better concealment. A strong rashness was in him, more of the feeling of three nights ago when he and Frank had brawled in the Paradise. He kept to the walk until he came to the first stores and there turned back to the alley that ran behind the livery corral at the center of town. Jim Faunce would never suspect him of coming here to get a horse, he decided.

He had taken down the two top poles of the livery-corral gate and was swinging a leg over the next, stepping into the corral, when Jim Faunce's voice drawled out of the deep shadow along the barn wall close by. "Been expectin' you, Stiles. What took you so long?" And, as Ned wheeled sharply to face him, he added, "I wouldn't run if I was you!"

The helplessness that turned Ned rigid was heightened by the prod of Harmon's gun at his belt. He couldn't see Faunce.

But he understood that the marshal had a gun lined on him. And in that moment all his sultry scorn toward Phenego's bought lawman crowded up in him. Yet he could think of nothing to say.

After a long pause Faunce's voice came again. "Step right on inside, Stiles. The front door's locked and we'll have the place to ourselves."

Walking in toward the high double doors, Ned sensed quickly that something unlooked for was about to happen. There was a quality of confidence in Faunce's tone he'd never noticed before.

He heard a step behind him as he reached for the small door set in the face of the big one at the end of the barn runway. "Straight in," Faunce drawled, close at hand. "We'll even have a light."

The harsh glare of the lantern hanging from a peg on a post to the left of the runway momentarily blinded Ned as he stepped in out of the darkness. He went on three steps and then swung slowly around as his eyes became accustomed to the light.

Jim Faunce stood there, reaching back with a boot to kick the small door shut. His gun hung low along his thigh in its holster. He smiled crookedly as Ned's glance dropped to the weapon.

He drawled evenly, startlingly, "You must be packin' an iron, Stiles. Go for it when you feel like it." So saying, he spread his boots apart and his spare frame hunched over a trifle in the attitude of a man cocked for trouble.

All this was coming so fast that Ned couldn't grasp it. Here was Jim Faunce, a man he'd have sworn never gave another an even break, inviting a shoot-out. More than that, the shifty look in the marshal's eyes had been replaced by another, a cool confidence that was disturbingly genuine.

"Go on!" Faunce rasped. All at once his hands lifted to the buckle of his sagging shell belt. He uncinched it and swung belt and holster to the side, dropping them. "Or do you want it this way?"

Ned queried flatly, "What is this, Faunce, an arrest?"

"Arrest be damned! You've been ridin' me ever since you laid eyes on me. Right now I'm askin' to see what you've got to back it up!"

Ned smiled broadly. "You been drinkin' turpentine?" he drawled.

When Faunce made no reply, Ned

pulled his coat open and peeled it off. He forgot Harmon's gun until his hand brushed against it. He lifted it from his belt and tossed it over into the straw of the end stall. Up along the runway a horse snorted and stamped heavily against the stall planking and the sound boomed hollowly down the runway to heighten the stillness. He could hear Faunce's short labored breathing that spoke plainly of the tension in him that didn't show on his face.

"Maybe you didn't sell out all your guts after all," Ned said tonelessly as he advanced a step and put Faunce almost within reach. "We'll see."

He had been intending to throw the first blow and had spoken intentionally to heighten the surprise of the uppercut he was balanced on the toes of his boots to swing. But suddenly Faunce lashed out with both fists. Ned ducked the right, ducked his head straight into the marshal's hard left. It caught him solidly on the shelf of his jaw and tilted his head back and took the spring out of his knees. Before he could recover, Faunce's left slammed in at his ribs, driving the wind from his lungs.

Ned stepped back gagging for air, bringing his hands up to cover his face. Another blow numbed his forearm and he struck out wildly with his right. It glanced off Faunce's shoulder but drove the marshal back a step. In that brief second's respite, Ned got his breath and the fog of Faunce's first punch cleared from his brain.

Stepping aside nimbly, he crowded in on the marshal. His quick-timed feint didn't draw Faunce off balance so that the blow he struck missed completely. Faunce hit him twice before he moved away, once full in the lips. He felt the salty taste of blood in his mouth as the marshal pressed his advantage. His anger came in an engulfing hot wave and he forgot what little science he knew of fighting and waded in slugging. They stood toe to toe, throwing wild blows, a few that connected. Suddenly one of Ned's told, catching Faunce on the point of the chin and driving him backward so that he tripped over the high sawhorse saddle pole and brought it down with him in his fall, spilling half a dozen saddles.

Ned pressed home his advantage, casting aside all ethics as he swung a boot at Faunce. The marshal rolled out of the way barely in time, caught Ned's boot and dragged him off his feet. Ned tried to fall on Faunce but missed. A bright spattering of light cut through his brain as Faunce brought his elbow down hard across his face. He struck out wildly, blindly, trying to hit the marshal. But Faunce had rolled clear and was on his feet. He had the chance to kick Ned's ribs in but didn't take it. Ned, groggy, got to his knees and tried to stand up. He was barely managing it when Faunce hit him on the ear and knocked him down again.

Helpless rage was crowding Ned as he rolled in behind a leg of the overturned sawhorse, thinking Faunce would come after him. But Faunce made no move at him. The marshal stood head down, boots spread wide, his flat chest heaving with his labored breathing. His straight black hair had fallen down into his eyes and blood streamed from his nose as far down as his chin.

Faunce asked, "Enough?"

But Ned shook his head and gathered his feet under him. The next instant he was lunging erect, lifting the big sawhorse with him. He tilted it up and over, trying to throw it at Faunce. It was too heavy and crashed to the floor as Faunce side-stepped. Ned rushed the marshal. But his legs were unsteady and when he missed his punch he lurched into Faunce. Faunce brought his knee up into Ned's groin and backed away as Ned groaned.

Ned saw the next blow coming, a hard uppercut that began at the level of Faunce's knees. He whirled around and took the blow on his back and then pushed hard backward to drive Faunce off his feet. They fell that way, Ned's head snapping back into Faunce's face as they hit the floor.

Ned felt the marshal's thin frame go loose under him. He held himself rigid before the expected slam of Faunce's fists. But Faunce made no move. Presently, when he could summon the strength, Ned rolled over and onto his knees and stared down at Faunce. The marshal lay loosely sprawled, eyes open and staring sightlessly overhead. He was taking in deep quick breaths. He was unconscious, having been knocked out when his head snapped back against the planking.

For a long moment Ned looked down at him, feeling the blood that bathed his chin from his cut and swollen lips. Finally a soft chuckle escaped his heaving chest. It grew into a prolonged laugh.

When he sobered, his glance was tinged with astonishment. "Got his goat, I did," he breathed as he looked down at the unconscious man. "By God, he had me licked!"

He stood up but couldn't trust himself to walk over and pick up his Stetson for several moments, until the weakness went out of his legs. But after he had gone over and clamped the felt on his brick-red hair, and picked up his gun, he came back to stare down at Faunce again, uncomprehendingly.

"He's a tough son of a gun and he never let on," he breathed, half aloud. "I'd sure as hell like to know why!"

He went out into the corral and cut out a horse, coming in again to pick a saddle from those lying on the floor near the sawhorse. Had he taken the trouble to walk back to where Faunce lay, he would have seen that the marshal's eyes no longer stared sightlessly loftward but were following his every move.

Once Ned had lugged the saddle out through the door, Faunce sat up. For a moment he held his aching head in his hands. Then, as he heard Ned pulling down the bars of the corral gate, he came uncertainly to his feet and moved toward the door. He ignored his gun as he walked past it.

He got to the door in time to see Ned swing into the livery pony's saddle and head up the alley. He stepped out into the darkness so as to see better and stood there until Ned crossed the outwash of light from a store's rear lean-to two dozen rods farther on. That alley led to the Jimtown road.

He went back into the barn and picked up his gun. There was a distorted yet proud smile on his face as he walked the length of the runway and through the small door at the head of it out onto the walk.

Two minutes later he was entering Phenego's office by way of the alley entrance. Without preliminary he told Phenego, "Stiles got away."

Phenego was staring at him quizzically. "Looks like he run into you before he left," he drawled. He would have smiled but for an unfamiliar truculent light in the lawman's eye.

"He's headed for Jimtown, in case

you're interested," Faunce went on, ignoring the remark.

"Should I be?"

"Maybe not." Faunce's tone was clipped. He reached up and unpinned the circled metal shield from his vest pocket. He tossed the badge to the desk. "I'm through, tired of this stinkin' mess! I was through this afternoon when Osgood and I busted into the Le Soeur house and found the girl gone."

Phenego's face flushed darkly. "Watch your tongue, Faunce!"

Again Faunce went on speaking in plain disregard of the saloonman's words. "I'd like to stick around and see Justice collect your scalp." He opened the alley door. "On second thought, maybe I will."

Phenego stood wordless and staring in bridled fury at the closing door. Yesterday or even this morning he would have found a way to quickly end this mutiny in an understrapper, particularly in Jim Faunce. So it was something of a tribute to the change in Faunce that he was now at a loss.

Slowly, as anger left him, Phenego began to attach significance to Faunce's mention of Stiles. The muted din of the saloon abruptly became a nerve-wearing clamor that irritated him; he was so immune to it that he rarely gave it notice, but tonight it grated against his nerves and he was distinctly aware of the oppressive staleness of the office's foul air.

He made a sudden decision that sent him to the inner door, where he signaled the houseman on the dance floor. "Tell Cliff to go saddle me a horse and bring it around to the alley," he told the man, ignoring the faint questioning look that met his words.

Ten minutes later Phenego was riding out the alley, a solid ungraceful shape on a scrubby horse. He was playing the still vague hunch that Jim Faunce had put him onto something that might give him one answer of the many he needed—the answers to who had kidnapped Belle Le Soeur, who had relieved Richter of the Wells-Fargo wallet.

The feel of the saddle was strange to him. He was headed for Jimtown; he was alone.

XV

ROY MOREFORD took a deliberate step out from the bar of the Jimtown saloon. His move placed him so that he was looking down on Tex Brandt, who had a moment ago drawled that rash challenge into the room's stillness. It also kept the stranger within his line of vision. He suspected that the stranger was this Frank Justice they'd been hearing about.

He said tonelessly, "Tex, you've got a loose mouth." He looked across at the stranger, nodding to indicate Tex. "He's had one drink. Give him two and he'd feel big enough to lick me." He gave a booming laugh.

The grave expression on Frank's face didn't change, nor did the cold regard of his gray eyes. He waited until the echo of the big man's laughter had faded, then drawled, "We were speakin' of Belle Le Soeur. Where have you hid her?"

Roy Moreford was carefully considering a reply. He'd had little sleep in the last thirty-six hours and his patience was worn thin. After a job like the one they'd just finished, it was natural that Brandt and Huston should hit the bottle. They weren't in such good shape to handle a ticklish situation like this. Charley, the barkeep, wasn't either, being naturally so cantankerous and suspicious that he was unfriendly to any stranger coming in the place, and there weren't many who did come.

He was about to give Justice his reply when Tex Brandt spoke first.

"What's it worth if we tell you?" was what Tex said, and he stepped past Moreford and down the bar toward Justice.

Moreford boomed, "Hold it, Tex!" but was too late.

Frank Justice's hand was already lifting along his thigh. In the split-second upswing of the .38 Roy Moreford was thankful that it was Tex, not he, who faced the gun. Tex was trying and made a stab toward holster. But Roy Moreford had never seen a draw as smooth and blurred-fast as Justice's; yes, one other, maybe, for he'd been on the street three nights ago and seen Ed Brice draw on Mountain's crew. He thought for an instant that Justice was going to shoot. So did Huston; for he lunged out of line with Tex, being jarred nearly off his feet as he collided with Moreford.

But the upswing of Frank's .38 didn't break until it was head-high. Then it arced down and caught the dodging Tex Brandt hard on the temple. Brandt went down, to his knees, onto his face, his gun's sight barely clear of leather.

Frank ignored the man lying at his feet. "Do you take me to the girl or do I go ahead?" he said.

"Easy, friend," Roy Moreford drawled, and his smile didn't mask his high-running wariness. "I told you Tex was drunk."

He might have forestalled what he was sure now was coming. But Charley, behind the bar, spoiled whatever chance he had. Charley had seen enough to know a game of keeps when he saw it. He hadn't moved since this had started. He hadn't had to; for he was standing in the right place, with the lamp right above his head.

Charley's hands slowly came up. The gesture was a natural one in the face of Frank's drawn gun. But suddenly he reached overhead and swept the lamp from its bracket. Then he dived behind his bar.

The scant second it took the lamp to

fall was an interval Roy Moreford thought would never end. He stood stock-still, not moving his hands, knowing it was his only defense against Justice's drawn gun. Huston lost his head, wheeling sideward and going for his .45. Frank's gun exploded in a deafening concussion at the exact instant Tex Brandt's swinging boot caught him on the shin.

Before the lamp's crash threw the room into sudden total darkness, Moreford saw that Tex's boot thrust had spoiled Frank's aim. For Huston stayed on his feet, his Colt swinging clear of leather.

But the next moment, as Moreford sprang to one side, Frank's gun stabbed flame again. Huston screamed and Moreford plainly heard the thud of his body hitting the floor. Moreford hurried his draw and laid his gun on the flash of Frank's weapon. He thumbed two snap shots at that blind target, wheeling instantly out of position. In the sudden stillness that blanked out the sharp echoes of his .45 he knew he had missed. No sound came from the direction of the bar except for a barely audible rustle along the floor which would be Tex Brandt crawling to safety.

From behind the bar Charley called stridently, "Someone tramp out that fire!"

As he spoke, a flickering light came from the rear end of the bar where the lamp had fallen. Then, at Moreford's back, a gun suddenly wiped out the stillness. Into the pulsing air another spoke twice, its flash lined across the room from the bar head. That would be Justice, Moreford decided, and threw a shot well above and behind the flash. Into the afterecho came the sound of a rattling cough behind him at the far wall. Something slid across the floor and a man's pulpy and gagging breathing laid an awful sound along the room.

The light brightened and Moreford cat-footed obliquely ahead until his back was to the front-wall corner opposite the bar. He stood there turned rigid by the threat this room held for him. Sweat bathed his palms until his hold on the Colt felt slippery and insecure. His glance jumped here and there, trying to pick out a tall shadow in the growing light that would be Frank Justice.

Charley bawled, "God A'mighty, we'll burn!"

The light was reaching out redly now,

tongues of flame licking a foot above the bar. The back of the room stood out in plain relief. Moreford's wary glance held to the flickering shadows near by. He saw a vague, prostrate shape lying behind the bar's end close under the boarded-up front window. He dropped his sights onto it, then eased pressure off the trigger in fear that it might be Tex Brandt.

But now the limits of his vision caught another shape ten feet away, a shape that also sprawled on the littered floor. He glanced quickly sideward at it and his eyes whipped back to that other with the clear image of Tex's upstaring and twisted face sharp in his mind's eye. Tex's rattling breathing had died out now.

He had already seen the huddled body of Huston halfway down the bar's length. That left Justice, who had killed both his men. It must be Justice who lay there at the base of the window. There was a moment when Moreford's finger tightened on the trigger again. Then a nausea rose up in him at the thought of shooting a defense-less man; some clean and strong impulse, a last remnant of a good upbringing, made him lower his gun and call, "The party's over, Charley. Douse your own blaze."

211

"Too late now!" came Charley's crisp answer as he stood erect behind the bar. He looked out across the room and saw the two bodies on the floor, and an expression of astonishment came to his round face. He swore solemnly. "He had that look about him," he said. "Where is he?"

Moreford came out of his corner. "Here." He knelt alongside Frank and found him lying face down, gun in hand at his side. He rolled him on his back and saw the glistening red spotch of blood marring the blondness of his hair above his right ear. Frank was breathing regularly, deeply.

"Just plain fool luck," Moreford said as Charley came up to him.

"What was?"

"My droppin' him. I shot blind."

Moreford had to raise his voice to make himself heard, for the room was filled with the mounting roar of flames eating into tinder-dry wood.

The barkeep gave Frank a single cursory look, then reached in under his counter to take out a canvas windbreaker and pull it on. He cast a backward glance at the fire, having to squint against its brightness.

"Well, there's the end of somethin' I never did care much about. We'd better be travelin'." He nodded out to Brandt's and Huston's bodies. "How about your side-kicks?"

Moreford shook his head. "We'd only have to spend the night diggin'. Let 'em be." He looked down at Justice. "But I'm takin' Justice along."

"Justice? You know this guy?"

Moreford nodded gravely. "It must be Justice. There couldn't be two like him."

Charley came around the end of the bar and crossed the room obliquely toward the rear, pointedly ignoring the two dead men. Moreford picked Frank up and threw him over his shoulder and followed to the rear door. Charley was untying the reins of one of three horses tied to the rail of a low back stoop when Moreford appeared.

He said mildly, "I reckon I won't be a horse thief by takin' Tex's jughead."

"Help yourself," Moreford told him. "You ain't gettin' much."

He heaved Frank's inert frame across the saddle of a second horse and used his belt and a saddle thong to tie Frank's hands and boots to the webbed cotton cinch, speaking gently to the nervous animal as he worked. The fire inside had gained headway now and they heard the rhythmic pulsing of its hungry attack on the building.

Charley climbed astride his horse and stood watching until Moreford finished the job. Only then did he ask, "Which way you headed?"

"Up to the mine. Why?"

"Nothin'. I ain't, though. This country's had it in for me ever since I set foot in it. I'll slope across the state line north."

"Hadn't it ought to be south, Charley?" Roy Moreford's face was all at once pleasant under a meaningful smile.

"Nope," Charley answered soberly as he reined his horse away, "they ain't made it that hot for me yet. I know a country where a man with a runnin' iron can still make a livin'." He lifted a hand. "Don't take no wooden nickles." His horse had taken three strides out toward the sage-studded slope behind the street when he pulled in abruptly, calling back, "What's that he was sayin' about a girl, Roy?"

"Search me," was Roy's noncommittal answer.

"Tex seemed to know what he meant."

"Tex thought he knew a lot o' things."

"Well, so long."

As Charley's pony walked away into the night, leaping flames burst through the saloon's roof to cast an eerie glow along the disorderly lots backing the near-by buildings. Moreford could feel the heat coming from the building now.

He said, "We'd better get a move on, friend," to Frank, as though Frank could have heard him.

By the time he rode across the far end of the street, headed for the valley's east slope, the fire had spread to the two stores flanking the saloon and was casting a broadening rosy glow skyward. By that reflected light Moreford saw a rider come into the lower end of the street, his horse at a dead run. He rode quickly out of sight, more cautious than curious.

Matt Phenego topped the lower lip of the valley at the head of the Goldrock trail. Two miles below he had caught that faint reflected glow in the sky. Sight of it had put a strong urgency in him, a need for haste, and he had ridden hard.

He pulled his horse in out of its run and held to a trot as he approached the town. He saw that nothing would be left of Jimtown tomorrow, nothing but charred timbers and maybe a few brick chimneys and the smoking remains of the shabby empty buildings.

He was two hundred yards short of the street's beginning when he saw a rider ahead, far toward the upper end of the street, cross before the light and go in toward the saloon. Even at this distance he recognized Ned Stiles. He saw Ned jump from the saddle to run in and jerk loose the reins of a horse tied to the rail in front of the saloon.

Phenego's first impulse was to circle and come in on Stiles and have a try at him. On second thought he saw the risk involved; he couldn't hope to get close enough for a sure shot, and along with this came a hunch that, if he missed, Stiles wouldn't. He knew Belden, up at the Pearl, and in the end decided to go up there for information. Belden might know what had started the blaze.

He put his horse off the trail, heading for the east slope. He remembered the old road the mines had used before the new one came in and judged it lay off through the timber high to the left. Presently he cut into the trees and held his horse at a walk, in no hurry now. There were several answers he didn't know to what was happening here tonight; Belden might furnish those answers.

He saw the towering shaft house of the abandoned Oriole mine close above. Even at this distance he could hear the roar of flames. The reddish glow was strengthening and even penetrated into the high timber so that he could see clearly the ground that lay ahead. His pony's walk was muffled by the thick carpet of pine needles underfoot, as though all other sounds were being subordinated to that of the destruction going on below.

Finally he saw the cleared line of the trail ahead through the trees. At that precise moment he heard the muted hoof-thud of horses climbing along it toward him. To his left and close to the trail was a tangle of scrub oak. He made for that and came aground, reaching for his pony's nose to check the animal if it should whicker. The brush was high enough so that he knew he was completely hidden.

The sound of the oncoming horses drew nearer. He saw the blur of their movement through the leafy tangle of the thicket. Then, abruptly, he was staring through thinner foliage, seeing a huge man

217

mounted on a big-chested gray. The rider held the rope to a lead horse. Across the saddle of the lead pony swayed a man's head-down and inert shape. He recognized instantly Frank Justice's blond hair and brown coat. He saw the matted dark stain of blood at the side of Frank's head. Then the lead horse had passed out of sight beyond the thicket, and only now did it occur to Phenego that he could have drawn his gun and put a bullet through Frank's head.

Or was Justice already dead? That was his first involuntary thought. He decided that Frank must still be alive. Otherwise why would that hulking giant of a rider be taking him up the trail? He didn't know Moreford but suspected him for one of those men whose loyalty Frank had secured in some way as yet obscure.

The outcome of this line of thought possessed Phenego with but one desire, that of seeing Frank dead. He lifted a boot to stirrup and was about to go into the saddle when he saw Moreford through the trees and higher along the slope. With a rifle he could have knocked Moreford off his horse. He saw the two horses turn into the trees toward this near side of the trail. For a moment he was puzzled, wondering why the big man was leaving the trail. Then he knew. The branching that led up to the Oriole cut off from the main road there.

He left his horse tied in the oak thicket and started climbing afoot. He cut obliquely up toward the Oriole's shaft house, now lost to sight beyond the trees. He was breathing hard from his quick-paced run when he caught sight of the shaft house once more, close now.

When Roy Moreford unroped Frank from the saddle of the lead horse, Phenego was barely fifty yards away, watching. Moreford laid Frank on the ground close to a lean-to that butted the high side of the shaft house, while he led his horse in through the lean-to's low door. He reappeared after several moments and lifted Frank from the ground, easily throwing him across his shoulder.

Finally Moreford disappeared into the shaft house.

Matt Phenego stood for ten minutes peering up at the Oriole. Its high tower was silhouetted against the craggy rim directly above. Off to the right and higher glinted a light from the Combination's bunkhouse and voices drifted faintly down from there. Phenego judged that none of the men at the mines were asleep, with the spectacle of Jimtown's blaze to look down on.

Suddenly an idea struck him, an idea that seemed the final answer to the wiping out of that old and bitter memory he always associated with Trail. He stared up at the cliff face, seeing its uneven ledges of rotten rock and the steep slope of talus footing the two-hundred-foot drop. He remembered that the Combination engineers had dynamited a portion of the rim before beginning work on the mine's shaft, for the Combination sat directly under the cliff and there had been the constant threat of a rockfall. The Oriole was farther down the slope and he doubted that anyone working there had ever looked on the rim as a hazard. But it could become one.

He started walking back down through the trees, considering the idea in his cold and merciless way. His walk quickened and then he broke into a run. He was in that moment a man with a warped reasoning, with only one desire. It was the lust to kill, a lust directed against the only enemy he had never been able to grind beneath his heel, Frank Justice.

Ned bawled "Frank!" for the fiftieth time.

His call was lost in the thunderous crackling of the flames that now had gutted all the buildings at this windward end of the street. Sparks geysered a hundred feet into the air and, in the shifting wind, were whipped onto the roofs of the still untouched buildings farther down. Ned could smell the acrid odor of burning cloth; it was his own coat being scorched by the heat that had turned his bruised face a beet-red and matted his hair with perspiration. Somewhere back there as he broke his way into a building, he had lost his Stetson. His hands were torn and bleeding from tearing loose boards nailed over glassless windows. He had scraped his shin and bruised his thigh when he fell through the rotting floor of a roofless and empty store.

He didn't care. Down there at the unburned end of the street the dun gelding Frank had ridden this afternoon was tied with his own. He'd found the dun at the rail in front of the now fire-gutted saloon. Frank was here somewhere. But where? In the saloon? Ned had broken into and searched every other building in Jimtown.

He was afraid now, afraid that the shape he had seen lying on the saloon floor when the front wall crumbled might have been a man's—Frank's. The heat had been too intense, the flames too blinding, for him to be sure. But it had looked like a man lying there ahead of what was left of the bar.

He clamped his bandanna to his face and ran down along the street now, out of the scorching heat. He was dead tired; he was without hope. Not even the thought of Helen Moreford could blanket the feeling of a deep and terrible loss. Frank Justice was dead.

He climbed wearily into the saddle of the livery horse and took a tighter hold on the dun's reins and started out the down-canyon end of the street. He rode with head down, slouched in the saddle. He had forgotten that he had come here to see Roy Moreford at the Oriole.

He was near the lower end of the valley when a deep rumbling echoed over the faint sound of the fire. That ominous sound increased to a low thunder, coming from the valley's east rim. He looked off there and straightened in the saddle at what he saw.

Jimtown's burning buildings lit the scene plainly. A billowing cloud of gray dust gathered and curled out lazily from the foot of the rim to the north of the Combination's shaft house. As Ned sat looking, a broad section of the rim's face gave way and crashed down onto the talus slope with an earth-jarring impact. The thunder grew in volume as huge boulders rolled down into the timber, knocking over the jack pines in their path. An avalanche of rock and earth swept a huge wide scar down the slope below the rim.

Ned saw that the Oriole's shaft house lay directly in the path of the avalanche and an involuntary startled cry escaped him. He saw the shaft house crumble before the pounding slide of rock. It was as though the shaft house was a toy structure built of brittle cardboard. It disintegrated completely and the next moment was gone, buried beneath tons of rock.

Slowly the pall of dust at the base of the cliff settled, the trees off there becoming clearly visible once more. And the far echo of the thunder faded until it was still again, as though the night had been wakened and had finally settled back to its interrupted slumber. The Oriole no longer stood on the slope.

"Now what the hell could have done that?" Ned drawled, tone one of awe.

A rider cut into the trail ahead of him as he neared the valley's lower edge and the beginning of the Goldrock trail. Ned pulled in, letting whoever it was go on. He supposed it was someone from the mines, carrying word of the Jimtown fire to the camp below.

He wondered how he'd explain what had happened to Sam Osgood and Harmon and the others. He wondered if he could tell them how hard he had tried not to let it happen.

XVI

At first Frank thought he still lay on the floor of the Jimtown saloon. Then he detected a faint reddish glow and realized, with some surprise, that his eyes were tight closed against a light that seemed to heighten a burning core of pain deep in his brain. The pain became so intense that he could distinctly feel each beat of his pulse, which seemed about to split his head open.

When he stirred, a cool hand was laid gently against his forehead and a voice close by said softly, "Frank, can you hear me? You're all right. Try and rest."

The shock of realizing that it was Belle Le Soeur who spoke made him open his eyes. The slender oval of her face was close to his. Above it light gave her hair the shimmering quality of pale gold. Her dark eyes were tear-bright, and deep in them lay a warmth that made him oblivious to the pain in his head and all else but this girl's nearness.

She said, again softly, "I thought you were going to die." Her words held a prayerful quality that was awesome.

That moment in which Belle Le Soeur's emotion lay naked on her face became prolonged, one Frank found himself wishing would never end. In it he had sudden understanding of something that hadn't occurred to him until now.

He loved the girl.

Blended with his deep thankfulness at finding her safe and close to him was an elation at seeing in her eyes the same emotion that held him. Then, in an instant, what he had felt was gone before a presence that towered over Belle, one that cut off the light and laid a shadow across her face so that he couldn't see it plainly.

He blinked his eyes to clear his vision. When he stared upward again it was to see Moreford's huge shape standing behind Belle. Beyond Moreford were gray-blue limestone walls and the same rock ceiling from which a brass miner's lamp hung suspended by a spike driven into a rock crevice. He turned his head and saw that he lay on a blanket. Across the narrow corridor was a crude wooden bench on one end of which were stacked cans of food. Beyond that was a small round coal-oil stove. In each direction beyond the reach of the lantern's light the low-ceilinged corridor ran on into a bottomless and pitch-black void.

He saw Moreford smiling broadly. Then the big man's voice was booming hollowly, "You're hard to kill, Justice. Damned if I don't think you'll be on your feet in a day or so!"

Frank tried to get his elbows under him and push up to a sitting position. He was too weak and Moreford, seeing him struggle, reached down and lifted him and turned him so that he sat with his back against the wall.

Breathing heavily from the exertion, Frank looked up at Belle, who now stood beside the big man. "Where are we?"

Belle gave Moreford a look that let Frank know she couldn't answer. Then the big man shrugged and said, "You both might as well know. We're in the Oriole."

Belle murmured, "It had to be the Oriole. There isn't another place you could have kept me without being discovered." She looked down at Frank, caught the cold killing glance he gave Moreford, and added quickly, "He's been kind to me, Frank. They wanted to tie me up when they left tonight. He wouldn't let them."

That look of Frank's eased only a trifle as he said tonelessly, "I've heard about you from Ned Stiles. You're Helen Moreford's brother."

Moreford nodded soberly, as though the reminder of his sister was an unwelcome one.

Presently Frank asked, "What are you going to do with us?" He had drawn his legs up and was now hunched against the wall, judging the distance to Moreford's legs.

"Nothin'," the big man drawled, "nothin'

but let you go tomorrow after they send the gold out."

Frank pushed out from the wall with his hands, trying to get his legs under him for a lunge at Moreford's legs. Belle gave a startled cry of fright. The big man stepped leisurely aside as Frank sprawled helplessly on the floor.

"Better get some of your steam back before you try that," he drawled. "Keep on with this and I'll have to hog-tie you." There was no resentment in him, no amusement either. He even reached down to help Frank crawl back onto the blanket.

It was a full minute before Frank was breathing normally. When he was, he said, "So you're one of Phenego's men."

He was puzzled by the surprise that touched Moreford's eyes. The big man was a deliberate thinker, too deliberate for that surprise to be anything but genuine. He seemed to think it out for a moment and his face went inscrutable. "Am I?"

"How much is he paying you, Moreford?"

"Is who paying me?"

"Phenego."

"Oh, him." The big man smiled as though he was enjoying this. He turned

228

his back to Frank and went across to sit down on the bench. "Enough," he said. Then he nodded to Belle. "Better have a seat and rest, ma'am. We ain't goin' any place."

Belle sat on the blankets close to Frank, looking worried. For Frank's feeble attempt against Moreford showed all too plainly how his loss of blood had weakened him. She hoped the bandage she had tied about his head would keep the bullet gash over his ear from bleeding again.

Frank said, "We'll collect nine hundred dollars for running that bullion down to Alkali tomorrow, Moreford. It's yours, all of it, if you turn us loose."

Moreford seemed to consider this. But finally he gave a brief negative. "No deal. Maybe I've done a few things that won't bear lookin' back on, but so far there's been no double cross." With a short sweep of his hand he indicated the canned goods at the end of the bench and the oil stove. "We got food and blankets and the air down here ain't bad. All you got to do is rest easy and get turned loose in another twelve hours. Then you'll be free as the breeze."

Frank was holding his head in his hands,

eyes closed against a sudden dizziness that had hit him. "And pretty close to the end of our rope," he breathed.

"Should that bother me?" Moreford queried. "After seein' you blow holes through two of my partners tonight?"

His blunt reply reminded Frank of something. He raised his head and looked at the big man. "Two nights ago a gent with mouse-colored hair and a scar on the back of his right wrist made a try at me with a gun in the yard. He missed. I didn't. Do you know who he was?"

Belle put in quickly, "You didn't tell me, Frank!" but stopped as she caught the look in Moreford's eyes.

It was a bright anger, one veiled over instantly by a studied impassiveness. "No. Should I?" Moreford drawled.

Frank was puzzled by that show of naked emotion in the man. But what was more important, he could see that Moreford was through talking. The big man's loyalty could be bought—or, rather, it had already been bought. Still there were things Frank had to know and he tried once more. He sensed that Moreford had lied, that he had known the dead bushwhacker.

"How did Phenego hear about those

contracts?" he asked. "How did he know we needed Belle's signature to put up our deed as bond?"

Before Moreford had time to reply, Belle was saying, "It was my fault, Frank. Night before last, after you left me at the hotel, I had Ned leave me at Mountain's office. I wasn't going to tell Ed about the contracts, but in the end I did. He must have told Phenego."

Something she said made him stiffen and ask abruptly, "Night before last? How long have I been lyin' here?"

"An hour; maybe less," Moreford said.

Frank looked at Belle. "It was last night, not the night before."

She said wearily, "I've lost all track of time."

"I thought for a minute it was already too late."

"Too late for what?" Moreford put in suspiciously, for he'd lost the thread of their talk.

"For the bullion to go down tomorrow mornin'." It was hard for Frank to believe that tomorrow was only Friday, for too much had happened in the last twenty-four hours for him to realize it had all been crowded into such a short span of time.

Moreford gave a broad, almost pleasant, smile. "If you're thinkin' of makin' a break, forget it. You're in the third gallery down, close to a hundred feet underground. Don't think it wasn't a job gettin' you down here. The shaft's full of water to within ten feet of this level. There's enough to fill a lake. So you can't go that way. And you can't go up either. You bled maybe a couple of buckets, which ought to mean you wouldn't be good for that hundred feet of ladder. Neither's she," he added, jerking a thumb toward Belle and asking her, "You tried it while I was gone, didn't you?"

She nodded and for a long interval the oppressive and complete silence of this deep gallery was uninterrupted. It drove home to Frank his utter helplessness. Belle reached out a hand and put it on his and moved closer to him. The pressure of her fingers as they gripped his made more unbearable his guilt and responsibility in her being here. But for his stubbornness Stagline would have been sold long ago and Belle would have had enough to make her comfortable for a few years . . . until she married Brice.

He found all his anger strangely centering itself on Brice. It had been Brice who, in the final analysis, was directly to blame for their present helplessness, for this quick turn of affairs that meant the beginning of Stagline's ruin. The Jimtown contracts would be canceled automatically by the failure to make even the first bullion delivery. But, blaming Brice, Frank saw that it was natural enough for Brice to have carried the news of Stagline's new Jimtown contracts to Phenego. Brice naturally wouldn't have known how Phenego was to use the information. If he had known it, he would have done something to stop Phenego. For wasn't he planning on marrying Belle?

Frank wanted to be sure of the thing he had seen in Belle's eyes a few minutes ago. So he broke the long silence by saying, "Don't be too hard on Brice. He didn't know what he was doing when he—"

They all felt the tremor that ran along the gallery as Frank's words suddenly broke off. Then, from the left, came a hollow rumbling that was at first faint but took on volume quickly. It became a deafening roar. Frank came unsteadily to his feet, Belle's hand still in his, feeling the rock floor trembling under his boots.

Moreford lunged up off the bench, bellowing something unintelligible in the roar of sound that swept the gallery. Above the continuous rumbling noise, almost deafening now, they all heard the thunderous racket of falling rock down the walls of the shaft close by. Then came the tremendous splashing as ton upon ton of loose rock plunged lower into the water-filled shaft.

Frank had to reach out with his free hand to steady himself against the wall, so violent was the shaking of the rock floor. It seemed to heighten the pressure of his brain against his skull so that he wondered why it didn't burst.

It was Moreford who first saw the foaming foot-high wall of water rushing toward them out of the shaftward darkness. He reached up and swept the lantern from its hook overhead and took Belle by the arm and pushed her back along the low passageway. Then, one arm thrown about Frank's shoulders, he braced them both against the swirling drag as the water hit them. The thunder of the falling rock faded and all that remained was the gurgling sound of the water rushing toward them from the gallery head.

The first impact of the knee-high flood eased off. Moreford said curtly, "I've got to help the girl," and waded back the way Belle had gone.

Frank followed uncertainly, hurrying his staggering steps after the lantern's fading light. He smelled dust now, dust that made him choke and cough. He found that excitement and this terrifying threat of being buried alive underground gave him strength to move, to keep his feet against the rising swirl of water. He kept pace with the lantern's glow ahead. Presently it strengthened and he came on Belle and Moreford, waiting for him.

The thankfulness in Belle's eyes when she saw him approaching added fresh strength to his stumbling stride. It was she who came to him and put an arm about his waist as Moreford snapped, "Hurry it!"

Frank could feel the water relentlessly deepening. They came to a slight dip in the gallery and there he had to lift Belle from her feet and carry her as he went chest-deep in the swirling gray flood. Beyond, the water shallowed to his waist, but he could feel its slow rise and all at once stopped. The excitement and exertion seemed to have eased the pain in his head so that it was at least bearable.

By trying to outrun the water Moreford was only prolonging the final outcome, which Frank knew would see them all drowning helplessly at the gallery's end. When he saw what an effort the struggle was costing Belle, he couldn't go on. He reached out and gathered her into his arms, lifting her with a strength that surprised him. Then, before he quite realized what he intended, he was kissing her. She didn't draw away. In this moment, which he was sure was one of their last, he felt the overpowering yet futile desire to live, to prove to Belle that this was no shallow impulse of the moment but an enduring and deep-rooted emotion that struck deeper than any other in his experience. He tried to speak, to tell her all this, and couldn't.

Presently, her head on his shoulder, she murmured, "I've known it since that first day, the first time I saw you. The way you looked at Brice when he spoke to me that morning made me think it might be the same with you. Then I wasn't sure."

"You know now." He tried not to make his words sound pointless.

She said, low-voiced, "Yes, Frank, I know now. Hold me close."

Moreford's lantern was but a faint glow now, one that cast light shadows across Belle's face, turning it fragile and beautiful. Then, suddenly, Moreford's voice was calling, "Comin'?"

Frank answered, "We'll wait here."

"Wait! You want to drown?" Moreford shouted lustily. "There's a winze down here. It leads up to the next level. If you hurry, we'll make it."

Belle breathed a sob and choked out, "Frank, we have to make it!"

A lost hope surged alive in him. Holding the girl in his arms, he slogged down the low-vaulted corridor, boots spread wide to keep himself from falling. The light ahead strengthened. He was no longer aware of the pain in his head.

When he came up on Moreford it was to find the brass lantern hanging from the bottom rung of a ladder reaching down out of a yawning break in the rock overhead. The water was chest-high to Frank now. Moreford's face held a tight smile.

"Up you go," he said, and took Belle from Frank's arms and swung her up so that she could get a grip on the ladder.

She somehow managed to get a foothold. As she climbed out of sight, Moreford called to her, "There's forty-seven steps. Count 'em. When you get to the top, crawl over the shelf and lie down. We'll be along directly."

Frank waited out a long interval, until Moreford looked at him quizzically and motioned to the ladder. Only then did he say, low-voiced, "You should have let us stay back there. This only makes it slower, harder."

Moreford shrugged. "I'd rather starve for air than drown, if it's all the same to you." He nodded above to the ladder, and then his arm raised from the water. His .45 was in his hand. He shook the water from it and offered it butt-foremost to Frank. He said tonelessly, "It'll still work. You may want it later on."

Frank said, "Thanks"—meaning it, for he understood that Moreford was doing him a favor beyond kindness. Tomorrow, or the next day, when the air in that upper gallery became too foul to breathe, he would have need of that gun. It was the only way. Belle mustn't die a slow and horrible death. He thrust the gun through his belt and, at a signal from Moreford, climbed onto the big man's finger-locked hands and reached for the ladder.

Before he started climbing upward, Moreford called, "Better take the light." So Frank reached down and took the brass lantern and ran his belt through its bale before he started up.

Now that his excitement had eased off, he felt a return of that former weakness. He heard the prolonged splashing far below as Moreford started up the ladder and the water drained off his huge frame. He had an almost nauseating awareness of the long drop below as he climbed steadily upward. The winze was so narrow that when he stopped to rest he could lean out from the ladder and brace his back against the opposite wall and ease the strain on his arms. He couldn't see Belle above him and knew that he was taking more time at the climb than he should. He tried to think of other things, hoping he'd forget the bone-deep fatigue that was crowding him. He studied the expansion bolts driven in the rock to hold the uneven sections of the wooden ladder and tried to picture how the winze had been blasted down through the porous blue limestone to connect the two galleries.

Suddenly he felt an outward swaying of the ladder at his feet. A sharp report, like the explosion of a rifle, took on the splintering sound of wood. All at once his footing was swept from under his boots and he hung by his hands, two separate sections of the ladder parting in front of his face. A prolonged and awful scream echoed up to him. There came a thud that blotted out the voice; then a faint splash from far below, its echo blending with the throwback of that agonized cry.

The ladder had broken under Moreford's weight and Moreford had been plunged down the deep abyss of the winze.

It was the sound of Belle's voice calling down to him that put the strength in him to heave his tall frame upward, hand over hand, and get a footing on the ladder. When he could get his breath, he answered her.

Then, leaning back against the opposite wall, he moved the lantern around on his belt until its light shone downward. There was nothing down there but a pit of empty blackness.

He called, "Moreford!"

There was no answer.

He called again, louder, "Moreford!"

Still no answer. Twenty feet below he could see another section of ladder. But the wall between the section he stood on and that lower one was bare only for the expansion bolts that had held the broken timbers in place.

There were twenty-three rungs to the ladder in the reach above him to the upper level. He counted them one by one, trying to keep from thinking of the horrible death that had been Moreford's. He remembered that last gesture of the big man's, his surrendering of the gun, and in it he found his forgiveness of all that Moreford had done to Belle. He didn't bother to think of Moreford in relation to himself, for his fate no longer counted. Into the man's warped nature had been blended a streak of honor, the remnants of a code probably long forgotten. No one but he and Belle would ever know how Roy Moreford had died, how in the end he had atoned for a wasted life.

He reached the end of the ladder and climbed out of the winze and looked down on Belle, who knelt beside the yawning opening. "The ladder broke," he explained, and couldn't look at her. He felt the prod of Moreford's gun at his side, the side away from her, and drew it from his belt and thrust it into his pocket, not wanting her to see it. Then he held the lantern high and looked out along the gallery, seeing it as a rock-vaulted replica of the one below.

He knew that he mustn't let Belle think too much of Moreford's death, so he said, "Let's walk back toward the shaft and have a look."

A slanting heap of boulders and crumbled rock blocked the shaft entrance to the long tunnel, to deaden the hope that the shaft hadn't filled. He hadn't had the time down below to puzzle out the answer to what had happened, but now he saw it and told Belle, "Part of that rim must have fallen." He was about to add that there was no way out of this blacked gallery but caught himself in time.

It was Belle who asked, "What could be at the other end?"

"We'll see."

Only by having something to do could they forestall the admission of the fate they both knew was in store for them. Belle knew it; so did Frank. They walked back the long length of the gallery, past the winze opening and beyond. Within a few rods they reached a point buttressed with massive timbers that held thick roof and wall planks tight against the edges of the narrow excavation. Frank saw something odd in this until he remembered what Shannon had said yesterday. Was it only yesterday that he had ridden to Jimtown? It seemed like a month ago. Or a year.

"Accordin' to Shannon, this is what closed the mine down. This and the water," he told Belle, indicating the timbers. "He ran into the same trouble near his lower boundary. He called it a fault. The bedrock split open and filled in with rubble and earth. They ran out of pay dirt."

They came to the end of the gallery within a dozen steps. A slanting heap of loose black earth and rock shards blocked their way. A shovel's handle stuck up obliquely from the pile of muck, and a pick with a broken handle lay on the earthy packed floor close by.

Belle smiled. "We could try digging our way out," she said. Then she took his hand and sat with her back to a slope timber, the gentle pressure of her arm drawing him down to her. Her voice was without rancor as she said, "There would have

243

been so much ahead of us, Frank. We hardly know anything about each other."

"Enough." He was trying to ignore the pressure of the gun in his pocket, at the same time wondering how soon he would use it. He wouldn't wait much longer, he told himself. He wanted Belle's last thought to be a happy one untainted by the approach of death.

He could see that she was tired, for she laid her head on his shoulder and murmured, "Talk to me, Frank. Talk about anything. I don't know much about you, where you're from, how old you are. You've never mentioned those things."

When he made no response, she looked up at him and only then did he say, "Sorry, I was thinking."

"Don't think, Frank. Don't let yourself."

"Not that." He knew what she meant. "It's something else, something about Moreford I hadn't caught till now." He frowned and paused again. At length an expression of wonderment eased the webbed sun lines at the corners of his eyes and he almost smiled as he breathed, "When I accused Moreford of working for Phenego, he couldn't understand what I meant for a second. He tried to cover it up, but it was too late. Belle, he wasn't working for Phenego!"

"Who, then?"

He shrugged. "We'll probably never know."

Again he was silent. Her head rested once more against his shoulder. Presently he was talking, low-voiced, earnestly. "But he did *sabe* when I mentioned the ranny that tried the bushwhack at the yard the other night."

"I didn't know about that, Frank."

He went on as though he hadn't heard her. "Ten to one he knew him. He may even have been working with him. Phenego would have sent his law dog around to check up if it'd been one of his crew. But he didn't. Jim Faunce has kept out of our way."

"But it has to be Phenego, Frank."

He moved around so that he was looking down into her eyes. "Don't you see it, Belle? Moreford didn't work for Phenego. The bushwhacker didn't either. Add those two together. I'll bet my last dollar Phenego didn't kill your father."

"It had to be Phenego, Frank. Dad didn't have another enemy in this country."

Frank shook his head. "Blowin' the back off a man's head isn't Phenego's way. Nor would he sick one of his men onto a job like that, not the way things were. He'd rather have seen your dad's outfit slowly ruined, dragging it out as long as he could. He could have murdered him any time he chose. But he'd have taken the other way simply for the satisfaction it would have given him."

Belle asked quietly, "Then who could it have been, Frank?"

He didn't know. He was trying to find that answer when his glance went beyond her along the gallery. The lantern's light reflected brightly from something back there. At first he didn't understand it. Then he made it out as the creeping edge of a pool of ebony-glistening water. His pulse slowed as he realized what it meant. The water was rising; it had already filled the gallery below and the winze and now was relentlessly inching into this upper tunnel. It was even worse than that! He knew that they had climbed higher than the winze mouth in coming to this far end of the gallery. This was the highest point of this level, and the water was already in sight—which

246

meant that the shaftward end of the gallery was already filled.

He purposely let nothing of the quick terror striking through him show in his eyes. The answer he would have given Belle didn't matter now. All that did was that she shouldn't suspect the death that was relentlessly approaching.

So he said, "Who could it have been? I don't know, Belle." He looked down into the shadowed circles under her dark eyes and gently pulled her head down onto his shoulder again, drawling, "See if you can't get some sleep."

"I don't want to sleep, Frank."

"But I do," he told her.

"Of course, I should have thought!" He felt the rigidity go out of her and it was at once apparent that she was thinking more of him than of the answer to her question.

His eyes remained fixed on that edge of lantern light. The line of the blackish-gray water was well within the light now. He saw that the hard-packed floor within the timbered section of the fault was nearly a foot higher than the solid rock floor back there, which meant that it would be some time before the water

247

seeped up to the ground on which they sat.

Once again he felt the uncomfortable prod of the gun in his pocket. This time he couldn't put it from his mind, nor the thought of using it.

Belle's regular breathing finally told him that she was asleep. That didn't come for what seemed an eternity of time. The water was within three feet of them now, visibly deepening as it crept up the brief incline that marked the beginning of the fault line.

The air was cool, not yet close, but he felt a beady perspiration beginning to break out on his forehead. He sat for minutes trying to think of something he could do. But in the end the gun was the only thing.

He reached down to his pocket, keeping from moving the shoulder on which Belle's head rested.

His fingers were closing about the .45's handle when he felt rather than heard the faint sharp ring of metal on rock.

He caught his breath and held it. After a moment the sound came again, more plainly. It was unmistakable and came from back along the water-choked gallery.

His mouth went dry and he swallowed to clear his ears, thinking they had deceived him.

Then he could hear several rhythmic beats and he knew it could be nothing but the driving swing of a sledge on the head of a drill.

His hand came away from the gun as his glance swung around to the broken-handled pick lying close by. He touched Belle gently, saying, "Belle, we've got some work ahead of us!"

XVII

GUS ORTEN and Ed Nichols rode the Combination's skip down to the mine's G level with the rest of the crew beginning the midnight shift. Orten was a powder monkey. Nichols his helper. They unloaded their gear at the mouth of G gallery, a doublejack and sledge, a part-filled keg of powder, coiled fuse, and their meal buckets.

The skip dropped out of sight. They shouldered their tools and headed down the gallery, carrying the keg between them by baling-wire handles, their lamps groping ahead to light up the gray-black walls of blue limestone.

"Tonight ought to finish it," Nichols said as they made a turning in the tunnel.

He was referring to the work they were doing at the end of G gallery, work that had gone on for three nights now. They'd come down at midnight each night and set off charges to deepen the gallery head. Both knew that Shannon was playing the hunch on finding pay dirt before the lower boundary of the claim was reached. So far his hunch hadn't paid out. Tonight's blast would put them close to the boundary and Nichols was betting that Shannon would close the gallery in the morning without even bothering to have the crew muck it out.

Presently Orten observed, "We ought to be under that slide about now."

"There sure was some hell poppin' for a minute." Earlier Nichols had been nearly shaken from his bunk when the section of the rim above the Oriole gave way and hit the valley floor. "It's damn' queer them two things should have happened at the same time," he added. He had a theory that the heat of the Jimtown fire might have been reflected against the rim with such intensity that the rock had expanded and broken loose. He didn't bother to mention the theory to Orten, who was taciturn and inclined to scoff at his helper's flights of imagination.

They rounded a second turning and felt a slight downward incline as the gallery made a line for the Combination's lower boundary. Soon they reached the timbered-up section of the fault and shortly beyond it were unloading their burdens, Orten eyeing the wall of rock ahead with an eye to the best way of placing his charge.

He gave no directions beyond holding the doublejack at a certain angle, waiting for Nichols to hit with the sledge. This job called for teamwork. A careless sledgeman could break the arm of his helper. Orten, on the doublejack, had to instinctively feel the cut of the stroke and turn the tool just so to drill clean.

Nichols could swing upwards of a hundred precise strokes at a stretch. But tonight, as they worked that first hole, he quit at fifty-four and eased his sledge down to the floor and said, "Y'know, a lot o' liquor went to blazes in that fire tonight.

You reckon old Charley got any of it out before the saloon—"

He broke off as a distinct tapping sound came from the wall at his left. He wheeled slowly to face it, moving as quietly as he could, listening. The tapping broke off for several seconds, then came again.

Orten pushed him roughly aside and put his ear to the rock. The *tap-tap-tap* was plainer now. Orten moved quickly several feet back along the wall and again put his ear to it.

"It's right here," he said.

Nichols swallowed hard. "What is it?" There was a ghostly quality to that sound that made his hair crowd the crown of his lamp-weighted cap.

"Roy Moreford's in there, in the Oriole," Orten said crisply. He jerked his head back down the gallery. "Go on up and pull Shannon out of bed. He'll have to work fast. Tell him to send some helpers. We'll shoot through with a light charge."

By the time Nichols was back, twelve minutes later, Orten's shirt was sweat-plastered to his back. He'd already drilled one hole and was swinging on the drill at a second.

Shannon was one of the half dozen men

with Orten. As he came up he asked quickly, "You're sure about this, Gus?"

For his answer Orten held up a hand and motioned them all to silence. Presently they heard that muted tapping coming again from beyond the wall.

Shannon barked an order to his crewmen. In bare seconds another doublejack was biting into the soft blue limestone. "Go light," Shannon cautioned. "We don't want the blast to kill him."

One of his men muttered, "The big moose ought to know better than to sleep underground!"

"It's a good thing he did tonight," Shannon reminded him for they had all seen the rockslide crumble the Oriole's shaft house.

The sledges arced fast in the light of the lamps, the ring of metal a deafening din. They took brief turns with the sledges, for they were working so fast now it took a lot out of them. At least two of them had been among the few survivors of last year's cave-in in an upper gallery when some rotten timbers at the fault line had given way and buried them in a short stretch of gallery beyond for two days. These two worked with

253

grim-set faces and Shannon had to tell them when to rest.

Orten said finally, "This'll do," when the doublejacks had bitten deep into the wall.

The others stood back, breathing hard, as he thrust a length of fuse into the holes, then hoisted his keg and poured black powder into the first. Shannon scooped up handfuls of rock dust and tamped it down in that hole as soon as Orten had gone to the next. Orten cautioned, "Light on that, boss," afraid of directing too much of the charge's force inward toward the Oriole's gallery.

A nod from Orten sent them quickly back down the gallery, Nichols lugging the powder keg and the rest the tools. They saw the flare of Orten's match and the brighter flare of the fuses catching and broke into a slow run. Orten overtook them. They stopped beyond the first turning.

It was several seconds before they were swayed by the concussion, then were deafened by the first blast. The second came an instant later and on the heel of it Shannon ran back up the gallery. The others followed.

Shannon heard something he couldn't understand at first. It held a warning note, like the rush of wind through trees. He slowed his pace. Then he knew it was water, a lot of water, pouring in from Oriole's gallery.

He stopped and turned into the man at his heels, jolting him hard. "Orten!" he bawled. "Keep two men here and start drilling! I want this gallery blocked! There's water, a hell of a lot of water!"

When he faced about again and started ahead, he saw the water foaming toward him along the gallery floor. There wasn't much, but it was coming faster as his lamp cut the shadows up ahead.

Shortly he saw chunks of blasted rock littering the mucky floor ahead, then came within sight of a waist-high and jagged hole in the left wall. Water gushed out through it. His lamp's light struck deep into the pitch-blackness as he knelt before the hole.

He told a man who came up behind him, "I'm goin' in there."

"Careful, boss," the man cautioned as Shannon's head and shoulders disappeared.

Shannon kept his head up out of the

water, wanting to save his light. He saw something move far back in the hole and knew it was Moreford. He reached in and caught a hold on an arm—an arm surprisingly slender. He pulled hard and dragged Belle Le Soeur up out of the hole.

He squatted back on his heels, breathing, "My God!"

Her hair was matted wetly to her head. The sleeve of her blouse was torn away, revealing a white shoulder running crimson with a deep gash.

Shannon said in bewilderment, "Moreford?"

"Dead," she managed to get out over her labored breathing. "Frank Justice is still in there. Get him out!" she spoke quietly but with an intensity far more urgent than another woman's hysterics.

The water was rushing thick-stemmed from the hole now that Belle's body wasn't blocking it. Shannon tossed his light aside, took a deep breath, and thrust head and shoulders into the hole. The water gushed up over his chest and thighs and into his face. He felt the cut of rock shards loosed by the increasing pressure. Still he wormed his way ahead. Suddenly he could breathe, for the pressure of the water had slacked off. He reached blindly ahead. His hand touched soggy cloth. He took a grip on it and pulled. The iron grip of a hand closed about his forearm. He struggled to crawl back. He felt someone grab his legs and pull.

Shannon came sliding up out of the hole on his belly, sodden, his face scratched and bleeding. But Frank Justice, the man he dragged after him, was in far worse shape. The bandage had been pulled from Frank's head and a crimson streak ran down from his blond head over his ear and along the sharp line of his jaw. His coat was ripped and he had lost a boot.

Frank lay there a moment face-down in the water until one of Shannon's men dragged him clear. The knowledge that he was safe—rather, that Belle was—had taken all the strength out of him. The water back there in Oriole's gallery had risen fast. It had been almost knee-deep when the concussion of the blast geysered water clear to the gallery's ceiling. He had seen the water begin swirling in whirlpool fashion low along the wall and realized grimly that the hole was below the surface. He had made Belle stand by while he thrust his legs into

257

the hole and found it big enough to crawl through. His head had been under water as he made the trial.

Then, as he wondered if she could make it without drowning, the water had funneled below the top edges of the hole and had cleared it. He had decided that the safest way for her to go was head-first. There had been those agonizing ten seconds when Belle's body had blocked the opening and the water had risen over her. Then he had seen her drawn clear and plunged in himself. His shoulders had become wedged so that he couldn't move. The water had buried his head. When his lungs felt as though they were bursting, Shannon had dragged him clear.

Shannon spoke now, saying brusquely, "Let's get out of here!"

A man lifted Frank to his feet; another picked Belle up and started back along the gallery with her. Shannon threw an arm around Frank and half carried him, past Orten and his sweating crew, the long way to the shaft mouth. The skip was waiting there. They were stepping onto it when Orten touched off his blast that was to block the gallery.

As the concussion made the skip pound on its cables, Frank stiffened.

Shannon told him, "Nothin' to worry about. We're closin' off this gallery to block the water."

He felt better when he saw Frank smile and drawl, "About the only good I've been to you is trouble, Shannon. You've got our thanks."

Shannon replied, "There's no thanks called for. I'm thinkin' of my profits."

"Then the contract still holds?"

"If you can meet the bond."

"We can," Frank told him. He looked at Belle.

She read the meaning of his glance and said, "You may change your mind once you hear what happened tonight, Mr. Shannon."

"We'll see." The mine manager reached for the signal cord and jerked it. Before the skip started up, he added, "The cook ought to have something hot for us. We'll talk it over while we warm our insides."

He was shivering with the chill of his damp clothing and knew that Belle and Frank were thoroughly miserable. But all that mattered to him in this moment was that a brave woman and a man he had liked from the first were going to live instead of die. He sensed their feeling, the overwhelming relief at having been delivered from what they must have believed was a tomb. Moreford was dead. Something lay behind that. The news of Belle Le Soeur's kidnapping had reached the mine early this evening, along with word that Frank Justice was hunting her. There was the mystery of the Jimtown fire, that of the rim breaking away and wiping out the Oriole.

All of these things, Shannon suspected, were tied in with the amazing rescue he and his men had just witnessed. He was willing to wait for the answers, sure he'd get a straight story from Justice when the man was able to talk.

It was four-twenty when Harmon's heavy hand shook Frank awake. "Time to get goin', boss," the blacksmith said. "Shannon's rig is unloadin' the bullion out there now. Here, this'll help get you on your feet." He took the lid off a quart dinner pail and on catching the rich aroma of steaming coffee Frank got up out of the bunk.

The coffee brought Frank fully awake.

260

He emptied the pail, feeling better as the strong liquid warmed him. He had had nearly three hours' sleep and felt better for it. His head didn't hurt so much and he could almost forget the draw of the flesh wound along his head.

He stepped to the bunkhouse door and looked out over the yard. Across by the end shed flanking the back corral stood a hay wagon, mounded high with alfalfa. The wagon being here puzzled him until he remembered that Yates had yesterday ridden up to a hill ranch to order feed. No teams were hitched to the wagon, but he saw a pair of horses in harness tied to the rack by the water trough.

Beyond the hay wagon stood the stage and a buckboard Frank recognized as the Combination's, the one that had brought Belle and him down from Jimtown three hours ago. In the light of a lantern hung from the mud wagon's brake arm, Ned Stiles and Yates were unloading canvas-wrapped bars of bullion from the buckboard's bed into the stage. Two others, Combination crewmen, stood facing the front of the yard, shotguns warily upslanted over their shoulders.

Shannon had offered to bring the gold

down, collecting the shipment from the other mines below the Jimtown rim along with that which came out of his own safe. "You get down to town and get some sleep," the Irishman had said, and insisted on one of his crew driving Frank and Belle back to Goldrock in the buckboard after they'd eaten a hot meal in the Combination's cookshack and dried out before the big sheet-iron stove there.

Belle had gone to sleep with her head on Frank's shoulder before they had come a mile. Shannon had sent a man on ahead to tell Osgood that they were on the way and Belle hadn't wakened even when Frank, with the lawyer's help, lifted her from the buckboard and carried her into her house. But they had wakened her so she could sign the papers Osgood had with him. After that a neighbor woman the lawyer had called in took Belle in charge and put her to bed. Before Frank started down to Stagline's bunkhouse, he had seen the bond papers on their way back to Jimtown with Shannon's driver.

Now, seeing the Combination guards in the yard, Frank was once again thankful that he'd had a man like Mike Shannon to deal with. Back there in the Combination's cookshack, he and Belle had sat before the stove wrapped in blankets while the Irishman forced them to drink hot soup the cook had prepared. He had listened without once interrupting as Belle and Frank gave him the unvarnished facts of what had happened in the Oriole. He had doubtless decided for himself who was responsible for Belle's having been kept a prisoner in the mine, for he had commented, "Roy Moreford wouldn't have done it on his own. He was a little shy on brains."

But he did have one bit of information to give Frank. "That rockslide is botherin' me, Justice," he had said. "We're close enough under the rim so that we watch it mighty close. We even blasted part of it down before we started work here below. I may be wrong, but my guess is that this was no accident tonight. Someone started that slide, probably by pryin' loose a big boulder. It would take something like that to start it."

With Shannon's unlooked-for indictment added to the Jimtown fight and what little he'd been able to learn from Moreford, Frank had no doubts now that an attempt would be made to stop the bullion stage on its trip to Alkali. Matt Phenego had every reason to force this as a final showdown. If it hadn't been for the contracts Frank had gotten yesterday, Phenego's own stage would be carrying the gold. Another thing that would gall Phenego was the killing of Hoff.

Ned had appeared in the bunkhouse as Frank crawled into the blankets a little after one o'clock. His face was bruised and his lips badly swollen. He'd been hiding in the stable loft since his return from Jimtown. When Frank asked him what had happened, he had grinned sheepishly and told about the fight with Faunce, giving the marshal due credit for having nearly licked him. That had led to his telling of the shoot-out and the reason behind it, Hoff's betrayal and the loss of the Wells-Fargo wallet. The news of losing the Wells-Fargo money had been too ominous for Frank to take in completely. Then Ned mentioned his ride to Jimtown and his certainty that Frank had died in the blaze that had gutted the town. Most important of all to Frank, in the light of what Shannon had guessed, was the mention of the rider who had come along the road as Ned was leaving the valley.

"Whoever he was, he pushed the rim in on us," Frank had told the redhead.

But Stiles had been too worried about Helen Moreford's reaction to her brother's death to see the whole significance of Frank's discovery. He'd asked, "What'll I tell her when she hears about Roy takin' Belle up there?"

"She'll never hear about it," Frank had told him. "Shannon swore his men to secrecy. All she'll know is that he died when that slide hit the Oriole."

Now, as he remembered the loss of the Wells-Fargo money, Frank tried to think what he would say to Chapin. There was nothing he could say, of course, to change things. The money was gone, although Chapin didn't yet know it, and the Wells-Fargo account would be canceled.

He put aside this added worry and reached for his Stetson and went out the bunkhouse door to join the crew over by the corrals. Fred Cash and Harmon saw him approaching and moved out to meet him. Yates followed a moment later.

In answer to Frank's query concerning the hay wagon, the wrangler told him, "Steele got this far with his load last night.

265

He's down the street now, eatin' breakfast. He's headed for Baker's Crossing."

Five minutes later the Combination's buckboard left the yard and Frank was walking the narrow alleyway between the hay wagon and the stage, wanting to see how the gold had been loaded. Harmon followed him. When Frank swung open the mud-wagon door and held the lantern so that he could see inside, he at once saw the reason why the blacksmith had come along.

A long heavy box was bolted to the floor between the doors. Two wide strap irons, not yet bolted down, held this box rigid. But this detail was less surprising than the big slabs of sheet iron cut roughly to fit the shape of the mud wagon's side and door panels. Frank glanced over his shoulder at the blacksmith.

Harmon said, his tone almost apologetic, "I can take 'em out if you think they add too much weight. But yesterday I got to thinkin' about how much gold we were takin' down and how bad it would be if we lost it. So I bought some extra hack saw blades and went to work. There ain't a bullet made that can go through that stuff."

Frank straightened, smiling warmly, and drawled, "It's a good thing one of us has brains. I'd never have thought of it, Harmon."

Then a thought sobered him and he looked at the others—Cash, Ned, and Yates—who stood close by behind the hay wagon. He was gripped by an emotion he could hardly define. Until now Harmon had been a loyal but somehow ineffectual man going stoically about his work. Yet the armoring of the stage was definite proof of a startling inventiveness he'd never suspected in the blacksmith. It made Frank's throat ball up to realize how solidly this crew was with him. Ned had killed a man last night and run the threat of arrest, in the final analysis, because of his stubborn loyalty to the outfit. Fred Cash had stopped a bullet night before last and should be in bed instead of standing here running the risk of pulling his wound open.

He looked at the oldster and said, "Cash, you aren't needed. Better get back to bed."

Cash gave a twisted smile. "You go to hell, Justice!" he drawled, and his smile held.

"Yates, someone's got to be in the yard while we're gone." Frank gave the wrangler a level look.

"Hunh-uh," was Yates' sparse but definite reply.

As his glance swung to Ned, Ned drawled, "No, you don't, friend. We're all in on this."

Frank couldn't help but smile. There was something determined yet cocky in their refusals to be left behind. He said, "Then we all go. There's a hundred dollars for each of you when we get back. How many guns can we lay hands on?"

A search of the office and bunkhouse netted them an old cap and ball .44 Colt's and a Greener—both Fred Cash's—Harmon's six-gun, Yates' carbine and .45, the .45 Moreford had given Frank, and a rifle and shotgun from the office.

When Frank told Cash that the old six-gun would be practically useless, the oldster bridled. "Who says it is? I can knock a fly off a mule's ear at forty yards with this hog-leg. Don't tell me it ain't no account!" The same went for the Greener, he added.

There were plenty of extra shells for all the guns but Cash's Colt. As they loaded their pockets with ammunition, Frank started out from between the hayrack and the stage, where he'd completed his inspection of the bullion in the box. As the sharp stems of the alfalfa brushed his face, he paused and glanced curiously at the high-wheeled wagon. A strange look crossed his face, but none of them saw it.

Then he was telling them, "I've had my mornin' coffee. Supposin' you go down the street and get yours while I bolt down the lid of that box. We don't want anyone fallin' asleep and it's a long ride. I'll be here with a shotgun handy in case anyone comes in the gate."

So presently they were filing down the walk beyond the fence. Their steps hadn't yet faded in the still crisp air when Frank walked back in between the hay wagon and the stage and opened the door and got to work.

They were back in less than ten minutes to find Frank bolting down the steel straps that sealed the lid of the bullion box. He straightened and tossed the wrench aside. If anyone noticed that his shirt clung wetly to his shoulders and that the job of tightening the bolts hadn't called for so much perspiration, he didn't mention it.

Frank told them, "See how this sounds. Cash drives and I ride the seat with him, Harmon is inside. He'll keep down out of sight where he won't be seen. He'll have the shotgun. Ned, you and Yates are to throw saddles on a couple horses and leave first. You'll go out this upper end of the street and circle the town until you hit the road below. Yates will cross to the far rim of the canyon; you'll take the near one. You're to ride the rims all the way out of the hills, keeping the stage in sight the whole time if you can. I'll drive slow in case you have to swing back and ride out any offshoots. Does it make sense?"

Ned was quick to say, "Plenty. That way we have a couple of guns to catch 'em from above when they stop the stage."

"No one said we're going to be stopped," Frank told him. "But in case we are we ought to have the edge. Let's get started!"

270

XVIII

Two hours after the Combination's buckboard had brought Belle and Frank down from Jimtown to Goldrock, three riders headed out of town along the rutted canyon road at a steady lope. They covered the nineteen miles to Hank Williams' station at The Narrows in a few minutes over an hour. Williams, a sound sleeper, was wakened only as they left the corral behind the windmill and pounded away in the darkness. He took his .45 from under his pillow, pulled his pants on over his nightshirt, and went out to the corral. By the light of his lantern he discovered three sweat-streaked ponies jaw-branded with Mountain's wagonwheel mark. He saw that his brown gelding, the black mare, and the paint were missing.

"Why the hell didn't they sing out?" he grumbled as he rolled into his blankets again. He was puzzled over the errand that was taking three of Mountain's crew down the road riding relays at this early-morning hour, but it didn't keep him awake.

Into Mountain's station along the dry

wash across from Stagline's corrals at Baker's Crossing on the edge of the foothills two hours later, the three riders came with the dawn. Tolbert, the hostler, was already up and forking hay down out of the barn loft into the big square lot below, where a dozen horses were beginning to feed. He hailed the trio familiarly, saying he'd be right down. One of them came out of the saddle and stood behind the barn door and clubbed him with a six-gun as he came out. While this one dragged Tolbert a couple of rods away from the barn, his companions disappeared inside and presently emerged to cut fresh horses from the bunch in the lot.

They left the lot gate wide open when they rode away. Before the sun topped the low foothills to the east, they reined in and looked back across fifteen miles of desert.

One of them drawled, "Here's hopin' you dragged him far enough away to save him from gettin' cooked."

A black plume of smoke with a rosy glow at its base marked the Baker's Crossing station.

"Wonder why we didn't burn Williams out back there?" another queried.

"The word would have got to town too quick," the man who had spoken first replied.

"Ain't we goin' to touch off the Stagline camps?"

The third rider spoke up curtly now. "We had our orders, didn't we? They were to put the torch to our own barns, not Le Soeur's. And we're being paid to do what we were told."

"Maybe we're bein' paid *not* to burn Stagline out," said the skeptical one.

"Suits me fine," grunted the third, and they went on.

At Lonesome they had to use their guns. Ray Simpson and Fred Echols, who ran the station across the road from Stagline's, refused to give them a change of horses. Echols showed the bad judgment to go for his gun when one of the trio started for the corral. He got a bullet through the shoulder, and Simpson was a trifle late in dodging the gun barrel that beat him into unconsciousness. The Lonesome station's barn caught more quickly than the one at Baker's Crossing, for it had no roof.

Eight miles out from Lonesome the three riders passed a Mountain coach headed in for the hills. They answered the driver's cordial hail but didn't stop when he seemed to want to talk.

Dead Horse came next. Ruling, the hostler, wasn't anywhere around. "Probably rode in to Alkali for grub," one of the three opined as he and the other pair set about changing saddles for the fourth time in the last six hours. They touched off both the barn and Ruling's shack before they went on. And, as before, they left the corral gate open.

By ten they were in Alkali, having a drink in the saloon. At ten-thirty they boarded the morning local, headed west. They had sold their saddles.

Back at Lonesome, Fred Echols bound up his shoulder and roped the last horse to leave the corral by the blazing barn. There wasn't a saddle that wasn't being turned to cinders. He found a broken bridle, repaired it, and put it on the horse. He dragged his partner, Simpson, in out of the sun and managed to get on his horse. He rode hell-for-leather back up the road toward Goldrock. Sight of the black funnel of smoke that marked the Baker's Crossing station made him hold the pony to its fast run.

At Baker's Crossing he found Tolbert lying still unconscious in the yard. He ignored the hostler and rode past him and out past the now caved-in barn to the bunch of horses gathered at the windmill trough. He managed to catch one and get his bridle on it. Then he headed on up the rutted road to Goldrock to report to Phenego. From a higher tier of the hills he could look back and see Dead Horse station ablaze far out across the desert. That sent him on at his dogged pace, and gave him further proof that the three Mountain crewmen had been bought off by Stagline.

Cliff Havens had his orders, which were to take his men well below The Narrows, to pick a likely spot and wait there for Stagline's bullion coach. No one but Phenego had suspected that Justice would try to run the gold today. But Phenego's hunch had been strong; he'd put a man up the street to watch Stagline's gate immediately on learning of the rescue at the Combination. This man had come to the hotel to wake him an hour before dawn and report the arrival of Shannon's guarded buckboard. Then Phenego had summoned Havens and four more of his men and told them what to do.

The sun was streaking the top of the canyon's sheer west wall as Havens took the down-trail Richter had ridden to meet Hoff yesterday. The five riders cut through the clearing where Hoff had waited with the stage and were presently coming out of the brush into the main trail.

Three miles below they came to a spot that looked about right to Havens. Here the canyon's high walls sloped up, not sheerly, from the narrow bed, almost completely filled by the width of the road. A big rotting outcrop flanked the road closely at a shallow turning. There was cover up both slopes, other outcrops behind which a man could hide, a few stunted piñons and cedars.

Havens sent a man around a higher shoulder of the left slope to leave the horses. Before this man was back, Havens and the other three had pushed the rotting crown of the outcrop from its broader base and blocked the road effectively with knee-high slabs of broken rock and a mound of rubble.

"That ought to stop 'em," Havens said, as the dust of the falling rock settled. He was breathing hard from his exertion, for it had taken their combined strength to overbalance the heavy section of rock. He took out his bandanna and mopped his perspiring face and looked up the near slope. He motioned to a near-by bushy piñon. "Reno, you can belly-down behind that," he told Reno Nelson. "That'll give you the closest shot. Wait until they stop, then shoot down one jughead. Don't any of the rest of you try for the horses. We'll need 'em to haul out the gold after we finish with their crew."

After showing the others the places they were to take—Ben Roerick in back of a higher outcropping, Dennis on a ledge that jutted out forty feet above, Haggerty behind a boulder on the opposite slope—he said, "I'll be here, close to the road." He indicated the broad base of the outcropping they had pushed the rock down from. "As soon as Reno shoots, stand up and cover the driver. When you see me step out into the clear, walk down to the stage. We want to be close and have every man under a gun before we cut loose." His bruised face shaped a crooked smile. "And I get Justice. Don't forget that!"

In another three minutes this stretch of

canyon bore the same desolate and deserted look it had twenty minutes ago. Except for the scream of a jay in the top of a jack pine toward the top of the far slope, there was no sign to betray the presence of Havens and his men.

The sun's shadow lowered along that far slope, tipping the jack pine with a lighter emerald. The jay stopped his raucous call. A rider came along the trail, paused a moment to survey the mound of rock blocking his way, then angled out and around it and finally out of sight.

Frank felt easier when he caught his first sight of Ned riding the canyon's east rim twenty minutes after the mud wagon left the lower end of Goldrock's street. A few minutes later he had a glimpse of Yates on the opposite rim and told Fred Cash, on the seat alongside him, "There they are."

The oldster nodded and eased the pressure on the reins and the teams settled into a faster trot.

They changed horses at the meadow below The Narrows, Cash explaining to Bob Aspen the reason for their early trip. Aspen wanted to get a rifle and join Har-

278

mon in the mud wagon, but Frank ruled that out.

Two miles lower along the trail Frank again saw both Ned and Yates on the rims, riding a little ahead. The sun was taking the chill from the air now and Cash was having a hard time keeping the fresh relay animals at a slow pace. Frank noticed the way the oldster's glance kept swinging from side to side, studying the slopes ahead. It brought back the worry he'd felt at having to expose one of his men. Harmon and Ned and Yates were safe enough; but Cash, the only available driver, wasn't. Frank had soberly considered driving himself but in the end had ruled that out, for it was all-important to have an expert on the reins if an attempt was made against the stage.

His hunch was that that attempt would come soon, if at all, for here below The Narrows the road was twisting and the slopes, boulder- and tree-dotted, offered good cover. The heavy steel plates bolted on the coach's inside added enough weight so that the swinging of the thorough braces was smooth and even. This slow pace called for a lot of brake on the downgrades and Cash rarely took his boot from the long brake arm. More than once the hickory brake shoe was smoking on those long descending stretches of trail.

The bloodletting in the Oriole seemed to have taken little out of Frank except that he lacked the high-running excitement that ordinarily seemed to lay a coolness along his nerves when he knew he was facing hidden danger. He felt no excitement now, only concern for the men who had come with him. Somewhere in the last two days he had lost the keen edge of his wariness. Regardless of what he felt sure was coming, his hand was steady as a rock and he eyed the cover beside the trail with no crowding instinct to flinch.

They made a wide turning in the trail and he saw the mound of rock and rubble that littered the road ahead and said flatly, "This is it, Fred! Can you swing around it?"

"Easy," Cash answered, and started lifting his whip.

Crack!

At the precise moment of the rifle's explosion Frank saw the off-leader's legs go from under him. The animal fell in an ungainly forward roll. His hoofs, luckily, slashed the air away from the other lead animal as the mud wagon rocked to its abrupt stop. A moment later the horse was dead and Frank was seeing Cliff Havens, his six-gun leveled, stepping from behind the broad outcropping forty feet ahead.

Frank said, low-voiced, "Don't go for your iron, Fred!" and slowly lifted his own hands as the oldster did likewise.

Havens was obviously surprised at this unlooked-for surrender. Frank, on the side of the seat toward Havens, heard the Paradise man breathe a startled oath, then call, "We've got 'em! Come on down!"

Looking up the slope, Frank saw first one man, then another, and finally a third step out into sight. He recognized only one, Roerick. He let his glance stray even farther upward and had a far glimpse of a shape moving in behind a ledge up toward the rim. Then his attention was riveted below as Phenego's men closed in on the mud wagon. He could feel the gentle roll of the seat under him as Harmon, inside the coach, shifted his position.

Now his nerves felt raw-edged and frayed. Havens' gun was centered on his chest. Behind him he felt Fred Cash suddenly begin to tremble. He tensed, expecting Havens to fire at any moment yet hoping Harmon's gun would speak first. It all depended on Harmon now; none of them could make a move until the blacksmith did.

Then he saw the derisive and scornful look that crossed Havens' face and knew that he was being given a few more seconds of grace. Phenego's man drawled, "Hell, we looked for a scrap!"—gloating over his easy victory.

The settling stillness was suddenly wiped out by the blast of Harmon's shotgun. Roerick was pounded back a step and spun around and fell sprawling. Havens' glance swept instinctively over to Roerick, and in that split second Frank moved.

As two of the Paradise men opened up on the mud wagon, he lunged back hard against Fred Cash, driving the oldster's wind from his lungs and toppling him off the seat. Bullets rang from the sheet-iron lining of the coach as Frank's hand stabbed down to his holster. Two more guns spoke, one close, the other from above. A concussion of air fanned Frank's cheek as he wheeled toward the Paradise men. He triggered Moreford's .45 once and saw his bullet catch Dennis in the chest. Dennis went down. Then, swinging his weapon on Havens, he heard the brittle crack of Ned's rifle speak from the opposite rim. Havens lunged aside and clamped a hand to his ribs. Ned's bullet had evidently grazed him, for he threw one wild snap shot at Frank before he glanced quickly up the opposite slope and dived in behind the protection of the outcropping.

Frank's glance swept around in time to see Nelson disappear behind a near-by boulder. Then, below Frank, Fred Cash's old cap and ball pistol sent a flat report echoing up toward the rim. Looking to the opposite slope, Frank saw a fifth Phenego man, Haggerty, go to his knees under the impact of Cash's slug. But Haggerty was only wounded and lifted his gun again. At that instant Harmon used the shotgun's other barrel. The buckshot tilted Haggerty over backward. As Frank vaulted down beside Cash on the mud wagon's off side, the Paradise man's body rolled the ten feet down to the foot of the slope in a smother of dust.

There was a two-second silence, what seemed a long interval of time. Then Yates' rifle sent racketing echoes down from close above. A high piercing scream came on the heel of the rifle's explosion. Nelson, caught from above, staggered out from behind the boulder up the slope, walked unsteadily a few steps, then suddenly folded face-downward to the ground. He didn't move after he had dropped.

All at once the two rifles up on the rims, both Ned's and Yates', laid a scattered uneven fire down into the canyon. Frank counted nine shots in all. Then from farther down the near slope sounded the beat of a pony's rattling hoofs. That sound receded quickly and was lost in a muted echo down the road.

From the far slope Ned called down, "Havens got away."

Frank stepped out from behind the coach, warily, his gun half lifted. Then he saw that there was no further need for caution. Three bodies were sprawled on this near side of the rutted wagon road, Haggerty's across the way making a fourth. Havens had managed somehow to dodge the bullets Ned and Yates had thrown at him and made good his escape.

In less than three minutes Ned and Yates came riding up on the mud wagon. Ned's battered face took on a crooked grin. "You sure called it," he said to Frank. "Anyone hurt?"

"No. But it ain't Frank's fault!" Cash growled. "Or maybe it is," he added. "The lead was sure flyin' up there." He was standing hunched over, rubbing his chest, for his fall from the driver's seat had knocked the wind out of him.

Ned said, "We can throw this horse into harness and go right on."

"No, we can't," Frank said. Their glances came around to him. His even drawl went on. "This mornin' while you were down the street, I unloaded the gold into the hay wagon. Steele doesn't know it, but he's sittin' on sixty thousand dollars' worth of bullion."

XIX

"You mean . . . ." Ned's jaw dropped open and he couldn't go on for a moment. "You mean we've got it all to do over again?"

"I didn't want to have to hold on too long if the odds went against us," Frank said. He was bleakly eying the sprawled shapes on the slope above the road.

"How about Havens?" Ned asked

285

quickly. "He'll circle back to the road. What if he runs into Steele and stops him?"

"How would he know Steele's carrying anything but a load of hay? Don't worry; it's safe enough." Frank nodded to the stage. "We'll go back and meet him. And," he added significantly, "we could pick up a shovel or two at the meadow."

They had taken the harness off the dead horse and were putting Yates' animal in the traces when Harmon stood suddenly in a listening attitude, drawling, "Someone comin'."

The others heard it a moment later, the sound of a horse coming fast up the trail. Ned reached in the door for his rifle and climbed the low bank to the left of the road to crouch down behind the outcropping that had sheltered Havens. Fred Cash picked up the reins and stood by the off front wheel, looking downward toward the near bend. Harmon and Yates went in behind the stage, leaving Frank standing beside the open door warily scanning the down-trail.

Shortly a man riding a lathered roan horse rounded the mound of rock blocking the trail. His left arm was thrust through his belt and they could see a brown smear of blood staining that shoulder of his coat.

He reined in sharply at sight of the mud wagon and for a moment appeared about to turn back. Then Yates stepped out from behind the stage, saying, "Howdy, Echols. What run into you?"

Fred Echols' wary expression eased somewhat. "A bullet," he said in a clipped hard voice. Then his shuttling glance took in the bodies on the near slope and he visibly stiffened. "Maybe I ought to ask the same, Yates," he said.

"We've had some of the same trouble," Yates admitted, adding, "and with part of your crew."

Echols' face was a study in bewilderment. He shook his head finally and said, "This is gettin' beyond me. This mornin' three of our Goldrock crew hit the camps down the line and put the torch to 'em. That's how I got this." He lifted his good hand to the stain on his shoulder.

Frank said, "Why would your own crew be burning their own stations?"

"Search me," Echols said. He nodded to the carcass of the horse lying in the road, to the near-by bodies. "What happened here?"

"Phenego tried to stop us. We're carrying gold," Frank told him. "You're on your way to see Phenego?"

Echols nodded, answering grimly, "Not that it'll do him any good to know. I reckon I'll mostly want to see a sawbones. You goin' to let me through?"

"Go ahead," Frank said. "Stop at the meadow and have Bob Aspen saddle you a fresh horse."

"Much obliged," Echols said, and it was obvious that he was much relieved to find that he could go on.

Frank was all at once impatient to get up the trail and meet the hay wagon. He went across to Ned's horse, swinging up into leather. "I'll go on ahead and find Steele," he told the others. "You can meet me above."

A quarter hour later he rode past the meadow as Bob Aspen was leading a horse from the corral for Echols, who waited near the tent. Steele was bringing down a light load and should be somewhere between The Narrows and Stagline's meadow, Frank decided. This morning before the stage left, he had suggested that the rancher borrow an extra team from him so as to make a quicker trip and the man had readily agreed. But as he climbed up along the trail and saw no sign of the hay wagon, a slow worry began nagging him.

As he came within sight of Hank Williams' Narrows station, he saw the hay wagon standing beside the hump-roofed barn, Steele pitching hay up into the loft. Driving boots into the pony's flanks, he pounded in off the trail at a run.

Steele saw him coming and thrust his fork deep into the hay and mopped his perspiring face with a bandanna. As Frank came up a guilty look crossed the rancher's face and he called down, "Sure sorry about this, Justice. But Williams offered me forty dollars for this load and I couldn't pass it up. I'll get you another down day after tomorrow."

The back door of the stone shack below banged and, looking down there, Frank saw Williams heading up toward the barn carrying a shotgun. So he deliberately drew his .45 and held it with his arm resting on the horn of the saddle. Seeing that, Williams stopped abruptly. He stood there undecided a moment, then laid his gun on the ground and came on.

"That's mine!" he called angrily as he

approached. "I've laid out good money for it."

"Forty dollars is a pretty stiff price, Williams," Frank drawled. He was paying Steele only thirty-two for the long drive down to Baker's Crossing station.

"That ain't none o' your business!" Williams flared.

Frank smiled wryly at the pulse-slowing thought of what might have happened if the rack had been unloaded and the gold discovered.

Williams didn't understand that smile and a darker anger gathered on his face as he snarled, "Ain't my money as good as yours?"

"Sure," Frank agreed, "so let's begin biddin'. Steele, my price is fifty dollars."

"Fifty!" Williams bellowed. "See here, you can't . . ."

Steele was obviously uncomfortable at being the spark that had kindled this flaring argument. He said, "I didn't aim to cause a ruckus, Justice. It was only that I was gettin' a bit extra. I didn't think Yates would mind waitin' an extra two or three days."

Frank wasn't looking at the rancher but

at Williams. "Well," he drawled, "do you want to raise the ante, Williams?"

"At fifty dollars?" Williams became mute in the grip of his anger and turned suddenly and trudged back down toward his shack.

When he stopped to pick up the shotgun, Frank called, "I wouldn't, Williams!" The station owner glared back at him a moment but in the end went on without his shotgun.

Steele said, "I'll have it loaded in a hurry, Justice. I oughtn't to have let you in for this."

"Forget it," Frank told him. "And don't bother loadin' again. The boys are waitin' for you with the stage down at the meadow."

Steele was puzzled. "Waitin' for me?"

Frank nodded, unable to keep from smiling. "For you. They want to run that gold on down to Alkali. It's buried down under your hay there, where I put it this morning."

He had to laugh at the bewildered and alarmed expression that crossed the rancher's sun-blackened face. His nerves, tight-drawn with weariness and fatigue these last hours, needed something like that to ease their strain.

Phenego listened to Cliff Havens' story with a slowly gathering look of impotent rage coming to his rugged square face. He rose and paced the office's short length with a choppy shoulder-heavy stride. When Havens had finished, the saloonman looked down at him scornfully, noticing particularly the small stain of blood on his shirt near his belt.

He grated savagely, "You get nicked and take to your heels! Your whole damned tribe turned yellow!"

Havens knew when it was best to keep quiet. Now was one of those times; for in a temper like this Phenego was merciless and cruel, better not prodded.

Phenego gave a grunt of disgust and turned from his man. When a knock came at the door and it opened on a houseman, he snarled, "Can't you see I'm busy?"

The houseman nodded back over his shoulder. "Fred Echols is here to see you. Something important."

Some of the rage drained out of Phenego. "What does he want? Why isn't he on the job?" Before his man could answer, he snapped, "Don't stand there with your mouth hangin' open! Send him in!"

He listened to Echols' story without once interrupting. But the news had its effect, for his rugged face paled before the awesome account of Mountain's ruin. After Echols had finished speaking, he stared floorward a long moment, seeming to study the high polish on his boots.

Finally his head jerked up and he asked sharply, "Cliff, who knew about this? Who would sell me out, hire my own men to burn me out? Who would have the hunch that I'd be so crippled after that try for the gold that this other would come close to wiping me out?"

Havens shrugged, searching for a reply and not finding it.

"Did your men talk?" Phenego asked sharply.

"They didn't have the chance," Havens said. "We went straight to the stables and right out the road. None of us spoke to a soul on the way out."

"Justice might have found out we were to make a try at him. But there wasn't enough time for him to buy off Brice's men. His own crew couldn't have done it. They were all with him, you say."

"We knew it and Brice knew it. Who else?"

Something Havens had said made Phenego abruptly stiffen. His look was one of bewilderment for a moment until it went impassive before some unnamed thought.

And just as suddenly his hand lifted in under his coat and came out fisting a pearl-handled .38 Colt's. Havens sat a little straighter in his chair. But Phenego had no thought now for either of his men. He opened the gun's loading gate and spun the cylinder, inspecting the loads.

He thrust the gun back into its spring holster and went to the door. About to go out, he paused a moment and looked back at Havens. "Cliff," he said, "do me a favor."

"Name it, boss."

"If you see Justice before I do, tell him something for me. Tell him I hate his guts. Tell him it was me that pushed half the Jimtown rim in on him last night. But it wasn't me that killed Le Soeur or had that girl hidden away. Walk right up to him and tell him it wasn't me. Can you remember that?"

Havens nodded and Phenego went out across the empty dance floor and into the crowd by the bar. Customers respectfully made way for him. On the street others turned and eyed him a moment after he passed. He remembered idly that he'd left his hat behind and promptly forgot that as he stooped under a tie rail and cut obliquely over toward Mountain's high runway. A heavy wagon's team nearly ran him down. He wasn't aware of it.

He found three men loafing in Mountain's waiting room. He told the clerk at the back desk, "Send 'em away," nodding toward the men at the front of the room. He went into Brice's office. It was empty.

He was turning to leave the room when a heavy step crossed the outer office. He moved swiftly behind the half-open door and drew his gun. When Brice came into the room, he pushed the door shut and, before it slammed, said, "Drop your belt, Ed!"

Phenego's voice and the sudden sound of the door closing made Brice wheel sharply around. His hand froze at his thigh as he saw the gun lined at him and the rock-hard set to Phenego's face.

Yet he didn't move until the saloonman repeated, "Shed it, I said!"

Brice reached around and uncinched the

low-hanging shell belt and let it and his holstered gun drop to the floor.

Phenego motioned to the chair behind the desk. "Sit. We'll need some time to talk this over."

"Talk what over?"

Again a nod of Phenego's indicated the chair, and Brice moved around the desk and sat down.

"It goes a long way back, Brice," Phenego said. "As far back as that first Stagline holdup, when Le Soeur lost the Wells-Fargo money."

Brice's face remained impassive. Finally Phenego said, "You might as well spill it. I know all but a few details. You had that stage stopped; I didn't. You'd have been the only one outside Le Soeur and Chapin that knew the chest was on the stage."

A slow change came to Brice's face. "All right," he drawled, "it was me."

"Go on from there."

Brice frowned. "On to what?"

"To why you killed Le Soeur and hung it on me."

There was a further easing of Brice's expression. He even smiled faintly, tolerantly. "You've made some close guesses, Matt," he drawled. Then he eyed the gun momentarily, noticing that it didn't waver. "Why did I kill Le Soeur? Because he had me in there that night to ask me about the holdup. He was suspicious; maybe he knew the truth. I shot him. It was right after I'd taken you up the back hotel stairs to your room. So I went back and put the empty shell in your gun and put your boots back on."

"And I was sure I'd killed him!" Phenego breathed, only the tautness of his heavy lips betraying the fury that was building in him. "So was Jim Faunce."

"You were both supposed to think you had."

"You cut Le Soeur down even when you were going to marry the girl."

Brice shrugged. "There was no way she could ever find out."

Phenego's thumb tightened on the gun's hammer, so galled was he by Brice's casual manner. In that moment he came close to shooting Brice but caught himself in time; there were other things he wanted to know.

"You didn't stop with that. You went right on. Why?"

"Nothing more would have happened if Justice hadn't put his oar in. I'd been

297

hoping you might sell me Stagline, maybe both outfits, once you bought out Le Soeur. The only reason you went into this business was to beat down Le Soeur. So I thought you'd sell once he was out of the way. I was going to use the Wells-Fargo money to give me a start and borrow the rest.

"Then Justice hung on and I saw it was to be a fight between you and him. So I let you go at each other."

"Along with a push or two from you to keep us interested," Phenego said bitingly. "It must've been Moreford that stopped Richter and got the Wells-Fargo wallet, since he's the one that carried the girl off."

Brice tilted his head in the affirmative, leaning forward slightly in his chair, elbows on knees. "Moreford and two men he picked up in Jimtown," he admitted. He nodded to the small safe in the far corner of the room. "It's all there—all the Wells-Fargo money except Moreford's share, which wasn't much."

Some inner amusement put a mirthless smile on Phenego's face. "So today you bought over three of your crew to burn me out, workin' on the hunch that Justice's crew would be cut to ribbons when my men held up the bullion stage."

"I was hopin' Havens would get Justice. It was a pretty sure thing, Phenego. Yesterday I stopped in at Stagline to see what they were doing to get the girl back. I saw Harmon bolting steel plates into the inside of a stage and knew the gold was being shipped out. It looked like it might be a close fight, with you maybe gettin' the worst of it."

"And I did," Phenego drawled. His cold fury was heightened by Brice's bland manner, by the almost boasting way the man told how he had laid his plans. "But there's one hitch. Justice wasn't cut down. His crew cut mine to ribbons and he came off without a man hurt." Phenego paused to relish the sudden wary expression that came to Brice's eyes. "It's a damned shame he isn't gettin' the chance to square things with you! I almost had that chance last night and didn't know it."

Brice's glance sharpened. "What chance?"

Phenego smiled. "Haven't you wondered who pushed the rim in on the Oriole?"

"You did?" Cold fury was on Brice's

face. He'd been half crazy with worry over Belle last night.

The sudden deafening blast of the gun he always kept hanging from a nail in the kneehole of his desk jarred Phenego's solid frame backward. Phenego's gun exploded wildly ceilingward as he gave a choking gasp. His head dropped. He tried to bring his gun back into line. Brice shot again, his bullet ripping a hole through the thin veneer of the desk's front face. He smiled disdainfully, twistedly, as he saw the broad expanse of Phenego's shirt front stir under the impact of the slug.

At this range Brice couldn't miss. Phenego, with a super human effort, once more tried to lift his gun as he tottered on knees that were beginning to buckle. Once more Brice fired, then again as Phenego fell. Brice stood on his feet. He looked down over his sights deliberately and sent his last bullet into the dead saloonman's brain.

Out in the runway, close to the office's inched-opened side window, Jim Faunce turned away and went soundlessly back to the street. His face was chalky; a nausea was gripping him. The last thing he heard as he came to the head of the runway was Brice's voice calling, "Go on back to work! I'll take care of this," to two men who had started across the rear yard, attracted by the sound of the shots.

XX

LAST NIGHT Jim Faunce's instinct for self-preservation had sent him to the livery barn loft rather than to his room to sleep. He hadn't rested much, for the fight with Stiles had left his thin frame sore to the touch in a dozen spots and his face swollen and bruised and aching. But, stronger than the physical battering he had taken, was a mental unrest that made it impossible for him to sleep. He didn't regret the break with Phenego; quite the opposite, for it had bolstered his newfound self-respect. But he was well aware of the manner in which Phenego dealt with a disloyal underling and acted accordingly. He lay behind the bales of hay at the front of the loft and when he dozed his gun was in his hand.

He had been up before dawn. He paid a furtive visit to his room, which he rented from a family that owned a house backing on an alley close in to the stores. He gathered together his few belongings and rolled them in his blankets and left the house without waking the owner and his wife in the front bedroom. At Slater's corral he settled his bill with a sleepy hostler, saddled his chestnut gelding and tied on his blanket roll, and had half decided to leave at once by way of the Alkali road when he changed his mind. No use in a man starting a ninety-mile ride on an empty stomach. He rode the alley to the lower end of the street, where the pound of the stamp mills was an ever-present jarring sound, and there ate a big breakfast of beefsteak, potatoes, coffee, and pie in a restaurant he only occasionally patronized.

At the restaurant he overheard two men discussing Shannon's rescue of the Le Soeur girl and Frank Justice. Then, as he came out onto the street again, Stagline's mud wagon had passed him, with Frank Justice alongside Fred Cash on the driver's seat. He knew at once that the bullion was headed out, knew also that he wasn't yet ready to leave Goldrock.

Curiosity was strong in Jim Faunce, almost as strong as his willingness to run the risk of staying in the camp to see the outcome of a feud he had taken part in. And in staying he wasn't going to tuck his tail and slink along the alleys like a whipped cur dog. He went back to the alley where he'd tied the chestnut and loosened the saddle cinch. Then he made for his office and spent an hour sorting through some papers, something he wouldn't have thought it wise to do an hour ago.

He was loafing in a doorway two doors above the Paradise shortly after midday when Cliff Havens rode up the street and went into the saloon. He saw the blood-stain on Havens' shirt and in that small sign had his first fragment to a pattern of trouble that presently started taking shape before his understanding eye.

It was some twenty minutes before Fred Echols also turned in at the Paradise rack on a tired and sweat-caked horse. This was the wrong time of day for Echols to be in Goldrock unless something of pressing urgency brought him. That much Faunce understood and read into it his own meaning.

Shortly, when Phenego emerged from

the saloon, hatless, his face set doggedly, he passed almost within arm reach of his ex-marshal without seeing him. Faunce fell in a few paces behind and, when Phenego cut across the street and entered the door of Mountain's waiting room, Faunce leaned against a convenient awning post and waited. Presently he saw four men leave the waiting room, one of them Adams, Brice's clerk. He read something ominous into Adams' going off duty at this hour and, on impulse, crossed the street and sauntered into Mountain's runway.

He was familiar with the arrangement of the rooms inside the flanking building and walked on his toes as he approached the side window to the office. Its top sash was open a good two inches and as he came up he caught Phenego's full-bodied voice saying, "We'll need some time to talk this over."

"Talk what over?" he heard Brice ask, tonelessly.

So he had stood there, listening to the unfolding of a mystery that had been, to him, no mystery until now. He'd misjudged Phenego, he saw at once. The saloonman had, compared with Brice,

304

been a much-misunderstood and maligned man.

Brice's gun cut loose with such suddenness that Faunce shrunk involuntarily back against the wall. He left the runway and recrossed the street quickly, wanting to put as much distance as he could between himself and Mountain's office. Gaining the opposite walk, he threw a look back over his shoulder and saw Ed Brice come into Mountain's street doorway. He pushed through the crowd, wanting to put himself out of Brice's sight yet having to stop and look back at the man.

Brice stood there, a tall and solid shape, glancing casually up, then down, the street. He took tobacco from shirt pocket and rolled a smoke. In the act of putting the cigarette in his mouth he suddenly stiffened at something that had taken his attention down the walk. Then he flicked the unlighted cigarette out onto the walk and turned in out of the doorway, stepping back out of sight.

Faunce's glance followed Brice's. He was a full ten seconds seeing what had caused the abrupt change in Brice. When he did see it, he caught his breath in a swift intake.

Down in front of Morgan's Elite, Frank Justice stood talking with Belle Le Soeur and Sam Osgood.

Frank had reluctantly turned in off the street a few moments ago as Sam Osgood hailed him. He hadn't wanted to talk with Belle or the lawyer, but it was a meeting he couldn't avoid.

When Faunce spotted him, he was telling Osgood, "It's on the way down. Ned and the others are taking it through. We were stopped, but it didn't amount to much."

Osgood read his own meaning into Frank's words. "Anyone hurt?"

"Not a scratch."

"Shouldn't you have gone on with them, Justice? I didn't look to see you back so soon."

"A little unfinished business," Frank drawled, and his look was enigmatic.

But Belle read something into that look and said in a hushed voice, "You're going to see Matt Phenego!" Her dark eyes showed alarm and worry.

Frank saw that he must tell her, even though he knew it would add more worry to that already there. "No," he said, his eyes giving a cool betrayal of his faint smile. "Brice."

"Ed?" Belle looked stunned, bewildered. "Why?"

He looked down at her with the last trace of his smile gone. "There's one thing I must know, Belle. He meant a lot to you that first day. What about now?"

"What are you trying to tell me, Frank?"

"Moreford worked for Brice." It hurt him to so bluntly word Brice's guilt, but it had to be. "I suspected it last night. Now I'm sure."

She closed her eyes a moment, her face going pale. Osgood reached out and took hold of her arm, giving Frank a quick and angry glance of accusation. Then Belle was staring intently up at Frank, asking, "Isn't there any other way?" She had seen the thonged holster low at his thigh a moment ago and now knew why he was wearing it.

He said tonelessly, "There's no other way." Then nodding briefly to Osgood, he added, "Take care of her, Sam," and turned and started on.

"Frank!"

Belle's call stopped him. He faced her again and looked down into her eyes and felt a sudden strange resentment in the

307

strong hold this girl had over him. Then she was saying, low-voiced, "Brice is the man you spoke of last night, isn't he? He . . ." Her voice faltered before she went on. "He killed Dad, didn't he?"

"I'm not sure, Belle. I'm going to find out."

The brightness of tears was in her glance. Yet she tried to smile as she murmured, "Of course you must see him. But I need you, Frank. Come back." She turned back to where Osgood waited.

Frank stood motionless a moment, awed by the thing Belle had done. In her few words he saw a barrier moved aside, the last barrier standing between him and Brice. If he had known this morning that she no longer loved the man, that the emotion drawing her to him last night ran deeper than that holding her to Brice, he wouldn't have delayed this meeting. He would have seen Brice this morning. But that didn't matter now. What did was that some deep instinct in Belle had somehow prepared her for Brice's guilt. She was letting Frank go on to face the man she had once loved, perhaps even try to kill him. As he went along the walk, a tall and grave-faced man, the trust she had put in him quieted the restless edge of doubt that had been plaguing him.

That doubt had been of Belle alone, of her attitude toward Brice. For, down the street a few minutes ago, he'd had final proof of his suspicions. Fred Echols, turning in at Doc Ralston's house to have his bad shoulder looked at, had spotted Frank riding in past the stamp mill and had hailed him and come out into the street to talk to him. He had mentioned the interview with Phenego and the saloonman's strange behavior after his cryptic questioning of Havens.

"You'd have thought he was settin' out to kill a man when he took out his iron and looked at it. Then he left," Echols had said.

"Where to?"

"No one seemed to know. I didn't wait around to find out. This shoulder's givin' me hell."

"You say he seemed to know who had burned him out?" Frank had asked the man.

"It looked that way to me. He was askin' Cliff all them questions and all at once hauled up short, like he knew."

309

"Try and think, Echols," Frank had insisted. "What did he say, exactly?"

Echols had frowned, thinking back. "He asked Havens if he was sure his men hadn't talked, sure they hadn't let the word out that his whole crew was going to stop your stage. Havens said they hadn't. Then Phenego said you might have burned him out only that you wouldn't have had the time to hear he was makin' a play for the gold and then buy off Brice's men. Then Havens said something about him and Phenego and Brice bein' the only ones that knew what the play was. Then's when Phenego seemed to know. I can't figure what hit him so sudden."

Perhaps Echols hadn't known the answer, but Frank had. In Echols' words he had found the proof he needed, not only that Brice was the only man who could have burned out the Mountain stations but that Phenego had stumbled onto the truth. Unbelievable as it must have been to Phenego, he hadn't hesitated. Frank knew he had gone straight from his office to see Brice.

His impatience at being stopped by Osgood and Belle hadn't been entirely due to his not wanting to face the girl at a

310

time like this. He had wanted to get up to Mountain before Phenego left so that he would face both the men he had been fighting since the night of Paul Le Soeur's death.

So now his stride quickened as he came in sight of Mountain's ramp four doors above.

He was that far when he met Jim Faunce.

The marks of last night's fight with Ned were on the marshal's face. But something else was there, something that made Faunce pale and touched his eyes with a guarded look.

Then Faunce was saying, "Brice is cocked, saw you comin', Justice. Phenego's dead."

Frank waited for him to go on, the news of Phenego's death failing to surprise him. When Faunce didn't speak, he drawled, "You've been stingy with your favors, Faunce. Why do me this one now?"

Faunce's swollen lips managed an unamused smile. "Who cares why? But this is on the square, Justice!" Then, as though he'd said enough, he added a brief "See you later" and started on past Frank.

Frank's grip on his arm stopped him.

Frank said, "I don't trust you, Faunce," and pulled him in beside him. "We'll double up on this," he drawled, and started up the walk pulling Faunce along with him.

Strangely enough, Faunce made no move to break away. It was as though the man had known he must play a final part in the violence he had helped shape and didn't even resent what Frank was doing.

They didn't speak until they were within two strides of Mountain's doorway. Then Frank pushed Faunce on ahead, not roughly, saying, "You first."

He thought Faunce might pause in that outer doorway. But the man went straight on into the deserted waiting room. Frank's glance shuttled from wall to wall, finally settling on the counter at the back. He said, "We'll have a look behind that," and his hand was brushing holster as Faunce went back there.

No one was behind the counter, so Frank nodded to the half-glass door to the back office. Grudging admiration was blended with his strong suspicion of the man as Faunce stepped calmly to the door and pushed it open.

The back office, too, was empty except

for the crumpled figure lying on the floor. The color left Faunce's face as he looked down at Phenego, at the pool of blood by the dead man's head, and he breathed with strange intensity, "Justice, you've got to make this stick!"

Frank stepped past him so that he could see into the room's side corner, giving Phenego's body only a brief glance. The back window that looked out onto the yard and the rear line of sheds stood invitingly open. He had drawn his gun and was edging in alongside the window when he happened to see something that brought him to an abrupt halt. It was the flat-pointed shadow of this building's roof cast midway the length of the yard by the lowering sun. What took his eye was a momentary break in the roof's smooth shadow line, a break that was gone a second later but that had clearly outlined a man's head and shoulders.

Brice was on the roof. He had left this window open purposely, hoping Frank would climb out through it and begin a search of the yard and give him a chance to use his gun.

He wheeled back from the window, glancing toward a second that opened onto the runway. It was closed, or nearly so. Abruptly he noticed a ladder nailed in the room's back corner. It climbed the wall and led to an attic opening in the ceiling that was closed by a hatch door. He knew now that that was the way Brice had gone, also that Faunce hadn't been sent ahead to trick him.

He told Faunce, "Thanks for the help. I take back what I said. You'd better hightail."

"Where is he?" Faunce asked, a troubled frown on his scarred face.

Frank jerked a thumb upward and motioned the marshal to silence. He said again, "You'd better go," and waited until Faunce had gone out across the room beyond. Then he quickly climbed the ladder and reached up to move aside the cover to the attic opening. It lifted easily and was unhinged. He moved it aside soundlessly and went up through the opening into the half-light of the loft.

He stood on the boards of a narrow runway that lined the center of the empty attic, his frame stooped under the low roof joists. He had a choice to make here. There was a small window at each end of the loft. The back one stood open, its

314

six-light sash leaning against the wall to one side of the frame. He saw something significant in that open window, as he had in the one below in the office. It was a plain invitation to step through and out onto the flat roof that formed the back half of the office.

But the shadow he had seen move along the roof line he knew must have been Brice's. He saw at once that Mountain's manager, having left those windows so invitingly open, would be lying in a position to cover anyone stepping through them into the yard or onto the roof. And Phenego's bullet-riddled body lying below was a warning not to offer himself as a target.

So he catfooted the narrow runway to the street end of the attic, kneeling there to work loose the two nails that held the window's dusty sash in place. They pulled out easily, as did the sash. He laid it to one side, then leaned out the window and looked above.

The roof's ridge was a scant three-foot reach above. He took off his boots. Then he hunched out through the small window, ignoring the long drop to the walk below. As he caught a hole in the ridgepole with his left hand, he drew his Colt's with his right. He came slowly erect, facing the long empty reach of the roof.

Brice wasn't in sight.

He threw his weight forward onto the roof. From his waist up he lay flat, his legs hanging back over the edge. He had wormed forward half a foot, his glance riveted back along the ridge, when Brice's tall shape came suddenly erect, throwing a gun into line with him.

So sudden and unexpected was Brice's appearance that Frank, his gun hand reaching to the side to steady himself, couldn't move for a split second. Then he hurried the forward swing of his right arm, knowing that Brice had expected him to do exactly what he had done, that the man had probably stood looking in the open window at the back of the attic as he climbed out the front.

He knew he couldn't get his gun into line in time and threw his long frame in a convulsive sideward roll regardless of the weight of his legs, which threatened to drag him over the edge. A terrific blow in his right shoulder pounded him back even farther as the hollow blast of Brice's gun exploded against the now faint noise from the street. He felt no immediate pain in his right arm. But, as he rolled belly-down again, he couldn't move it.

Brice's gun was dropping on him once more. He could see the sardonic smile on the man's face even across the fifty-foot space that separated them. Once again he threw his body into a roll, crossing his left hand over his body to take the .45 from his other numbing hand. This time he thrust out a knee and pushed in a foot farther from the roof's edge. The second explosion of Brice's .38 marked the exact instant he felt a searing burn across his hip.

He finished his roll on his knees and bent sharply to the side as he arced up his gun. Their shots came simultaneously. He was barely aware of the bullet's air whip past his neck as he saw his own knock loose a splinter from a shingle directly in front of Brice. He knew that the slug glanced upward, for Brice's wide shape moved back a lurching step and bewilderment touched his face.

Kneeling there, Frank took time to sight his second shot. Through the thin blue fog of acrid powder smoke he saw Brice go down. He got to his feet and staggered back along the roof slope until he looked down onto the flat roof. Brice crouched there, bent at the waist as though in prayer. A twisted grimace of pain wiped out the good looks of his face as he swung his weapon into line with Frank.

The two explosions made one prolonged roar of sound, the echoes beating back from the face of the sheds at the rear of the yard. Frank's gun spoke a near second before Brice's and the slam of his bullet into Brice's wide chest turned the man's weapon so that the answering shot went wide. Brice was driven backward in a broken sprawl. His big body rolled with the flat roof's downslope. He clawed out with his two hands, letting his gun fall, trying to catch himself. He failed, and his body turned over the roof edge in a leg-up fall. There was a moment's awful stillness before the dull thud of his ground-striking body came up to Frank. By that time Frank was on his knees, his legs having gone weakly out from under him.

He heard calls from below, a shout out on the street. He hung his head and his reeling senses steadied. He managed to get to his feet again, although he had to stand with boots apart to keep from falling. He pulled his right arm across his body and managed to push his thumb into his belt so that the arm had some support. He started back across the ten feet of roof to its rear edge, planning how he would sit down and lower his legs first to the flat roof below.

A man came out of one of the yard's back sheds and called something to him he failed to understand. Another joined the first and they ran across the yard and out of sight under the line of the back roof. He grunted savagely as he tried to put one foot in front of the other. There were closer voices now, voices that made him stand spraddle-legged and lift his gun again with the knowledge that Brice's crew might be taking the fight up where Brice had left off.

It was Sam Osgood who came through the attic's back window and onto the roof. Jim Faunce was close behind. Faunce gave the lawyer a warning look as they came up on Frank, for Frank's gun had swung around to cover them. Faunce saw the dull unrecognizing stare in Frank's eyes and snatched at the .45 swiftly—not an instant too soon; for the hammer snapped down on his thumb, its striking pin cutting the flesh of his thumb to the bone. He threw the weapon aside in time to catch Frank as he tottered forward.

They carried Frank down to Brice's office and laid him on the floor, where someone had thrown a coat over the grisly sight of Phenego's body. By the time Belle came in, Osgood had found a bottle in Brice's desk and Faunce had cleared the room of the crowd of curious onlookers attracted in from the street.

The raw bite of the whisky made Frank gag and open his eyes. He stared dully around a moment, until his glance rested finally on Belle. Slow recognition warmed the look in his gray eyes and brought a smile that eased the lined pain on his face.

He said, in a surprisingly strong voice, "This about winds it up, doesn't it?"

Belle murmured, "Yes, Frank. Or we could call it a beginning."

His hand lifted to close gently on one of hers. Looking up at her, seeing the unmasked emotion in her oval face, he breathed, "A beginning." He was silent a long moment as he studied her. "I like the sound of that. We'll make it a sure-enough partnership this time."

Osgood, standing over by the desk,

intercepted a nod from Jim Faunce that showed him the door. They left the room together, Faunce closing the door softly.

"That medicine ought to last him until the sawbones gets here," Faunce drawled. "Meantime there's some things you ought to know, Osgood, some things for you to tell Justice."

The mud wagon was some three miles short of Baker's Crossing when Mountain's upbound Concord rolled into sight around a lower bend.

Ned reached out and put pressure on Fred Cash's reins, saying, "Here's where I leave you."

The oldster gave him a startled look. "Where you goin'?"

"Back to see what trouble Frank's got himself into." Ned swung aground before the stage stopped rolling. Yates and Harmon were looking out the door to see why they had stopped. Ned gave them a grin. "Don't you three decide to hop a freight with that stuff."

"You go to hell," old Cash called down testily, keeping a straight face.

A new driver was on the seat of the

Mountain Concord, a man Ned didn't know. It was agreeable to him to take on a passenger, so Ned climbed up with him. As the Concord pulled on past the mud wagon, Yates called, "Say hello to her for me, Stiles," and smiled broadly at the look on Ned's face.

Ned admitted he'd been thinking as much of Helen as of Frank when he acted on that sudden impulse to take the stage back to Goldrock. He knew he should have seen her before setting out on the drive this morning. That feeling of guilt strong in him, he was impatient at the steady trot of the three teams as the Concord rolled up the trail, although the pace the driver held his teams to was steady and fast.

Later the relays were being changed at The Narrows in the last few minutes of daylight when Ned saw a rider on his way down out of the high-walled mouth of the upper canyon. He recognized Jim Faunce and climbed down from the seat and sauntered over to the rutted road as Faunce approached.

When Faunce had reined in twenty feet away, his battered face set impassively, Ned couldn't help but smile.

"That was as sweet a fight as I ever bought a hand in, Jim," he said.

Faunce's expression relaxed out of its tightness. "Same here," he said, and made a good attempt at matching Ned's expression.

Ned was after information. "Anything happen up there before you left?"

Faunce pretended to deliberate, said finally, "Nothin' much. Brice used a gun he'd hooked under the cross drawer of his desk to gut-shoot Phenego."

"Phenego!" Ned said explosively. "What the . . . Did it kill him?"

Faunce shrugged. "Maybe the first slug didn't. But Brice used four more, the last through the head."

Ned whistled softly. "Does Frank know about it?"

"He may, by now. He was passed out when I left. Chloroform. Ralston had to probe for a bullet in his shoulder."

"What's the rest of it?" Ned snapped angrily.

"Justice chose Brice. They shot it out on the roof of Mountain's office. Brice's funeral is set for tomorrow afternoon. That reminds me. You could take care of sendin' some flowers in my name."

Ned eyed this new Jim Faunce with a growing respect. "Is that all?" he asked.

"Just about. It looks like you might have to side Justice as best man as soon as he's on his feet. He's picked himself a wife and as far as I can see she don't object much."

"You're headed out?" Ned asked quietly.

Faunce nodded. "This country's gettin' too crowded."

"We could use a man like you at the yard."

"Hunh-uh," Faunce drawled. "You can have it, the town and all that goes with it."

When Ned said, "Here's wishin' you luck," Faunce lifted a hand and rode on.

Some ten minutes later, alongside the driver on the seat of the coach, Ned was saying, "I've got twenty dollars says you can't make town in an hour flat, mister."

The driver gave him a startled look, then reached for his whip. "Make it thirty and it's a deal."

"Thirty it is."

The whip's lash snaked out and exploded between the rumps of the leaders. Its echo traveled on up the corridor of The Narrows, blended with the rattle of the iron-shod wheels and the ring of doubletree chains. Ned settled back against the seat wondering how soon Frank Justice could return him that favor of serving as best man.